*Dedicated to my Pops, one truly
exceptional man and wonderful father.
I love and miss you every day.*

Mascot Books
560 Herndon Parkway #120
Herndon, VA 20170
info@mascotbooks.com

PRBVG0515A

Library of Congress Control Number: 2015903481

ISBN-13: 978-1-63177-095-1

Printed in the United States

www.mascotbooks.com

LOSING THE PLOT IN LA

SONIA FARNSWORTH

MASCOT® BOOKS

CHAPTER 1

NEUROTIC — PATIENT SUBJECT TO ABNORMAL
ANXIETIES OR OBSESSIVE BEHAVIOR... SCATTERED...

Rummaging through the mass of papers on my passenger seat, I caught sight of the notes from my last session with my therapist. *Last as in both most recent and final,* I thought as I pushed them under the seat to focus at the far more important task-at-hand.

On the hunt, I collect, cut, print, and tag every lead I could find—newspapers, bulletin flyers, internet print-outs, scrolled notes from promising bar conversations—nothing went untouched. As I haphazardly filed through the remaining stack to verify the address of my current target, I noticed a lot of repetition, and made a mental note to consider a filing system for future excursions. It might have seemed a little crazy, knowing full well everything was on the internet anyway, but all these papers gave me a sense of control and hope. I didn't want to miss the right one.

Many landlords were totally clueless when it came to selling the goods. Not only were the photos highly questionable, but the descriptions tended to be insanely misleading. They weren't necessarily outright lying, but Hollywood is quite the melting pot, and I was looking for bargains in neighborhoods where English was often the second or third language. Lots of things got lost in translation.

Ads that used the word "charming" frequently turned out to be miniature pieces of crap—the absolute worst. Charming equaled a dark, dank closet. When ads sounded too good to be true, they usually were. Even though I knew that, I got suckered in every time.

It didn't matter what I was doing when I found a promising ad—I could be in bed, on my way to another temp job, soaking in the tub— instantly, I was out the door, zooming towards that possible gem. You snooze, you lose…and I was in a cold sweat the entire ride, imagining the people who already showed up and claimed MY new apartment.

I got particularity irked with "FOR RENT – DO NOT DISTURB OCCUPANTS" signs. Here I was, winded, anxious, and excited (and depending on what I was doing before, quite possibly in pajamas or heels or wet stringy hair); there's no way I wasn't getting my instant gratification. I made sure no one was home, peered into the windows, and surveyed the grounds. Been there, done that…not recommended. Last time I almost lost my leg to a crazy overprotective dog.

I loved/hated looking for apartments. I got way too intense about it; the obsession set in, and I couldn't think or do anything else until I found "the one." It was all-consuming because most of what I saw was complete rubbish, but I KNEW I'd find it.

The mere thought of looking for a new apartment sent me over the edge—it was a complete adrenaline rush, which is probably why I ended up moving every year. My (suddenly former) therapist tried to dissuade me from cutting my session short this morning to come stalk this new prey. Listening to her whining about how I was just bored and constantly running away from myself without addressing the actual issues (how profound!), I realized that even if she was right, than spending money to see her every week obviously wasn't working. After some quick mental calculations, I abruptly quit Dr. Fix Me and sped off to spend the extra cash on a plush pad.

Address confirmed, I stepped out of the car and took a moment to admire how well my old, beat-up, black 1961 Jag MKII looked parked on this curb. I loved this car, even though it had seen much better days. The red leather interior was a bit torn and burnished, and gave it that yummy old car smell; it reminded me of the old Citroën my grandfather had shipped over from France. It even had tray tables on the backs of the front seats. Everyone told me it needed wire wheels, but I thought that would make the car look like a pimp-mobile. I liked the funky original hubcaps, thank you very much!

My generous Pops had wanted to get me a new car but I didn't like any of them; they all looked alike and were seriously lacking in character. I rented a car once and I lost it in the sea of identical cars. It took me two hours to find, wandering around like an idiot in the parking lot, pushing the unlock button over and over again. Too stressful! Someone couldn't GIVE me any other car; like my apartments, I knew I had found "the one" at first sight. Speaking of which...

The day had arrived. Turning around I knew I'd found it, my new home. The electric tingle of my adrenaline rush hit a peak, and I knew I must have it and I must have it NOW!

First off, there was a garage. None of that bullshit "off-street" parking that required fighting and praying daily for a spot somewhat close to home. This way I could avoid planning my entire life around parking.

The building was constructed in the early 1920s, so it was oozing charm and exquisite details, but I beelined to the most important room...

The bathroom. It was HUGE compared to others I'd seen. It had these insanely beautiful old floor-to-ceiling tiles in a really awesome celery color with black trim. It was absolutely gorgeous! The shower and tub were separate, which I preferred. I never showered; I lived for the full water immersion of a bath, and this tub was colossal, not one of those wimpy ones with minimum filling capacity. Why would anyone build a bathtub with the overflow in the middle, not at the top? Totally asinine! Let's face it; a bath was not sitting in five inches of water with your knees up to your neck. This apartment passed the critical bathtub evaluation with flying colors.

Since soaking was one of my favorite pastimes, the bathroom was a very important space in my world, as opposed to, let's say, the kitchen. Considering my specialty was chips, dip, and take-out, the kitchen was not a priority. Small, basic, and clean is what I preferred, and charm was a bonus, so these authentic black and yellow tiles were better than I could have ever asked for. As expected, there was no dishwasher, which wasn't a big deal; I actually enjoyed the Zen-ness of washing dishes, sweetened here with a perfectly placed picture window, so I could space out and fantasize about frolicking in the neighbors' pool while I was scrubbing away.

The living room wasn't enormous, but it had many windows and a cozy fireplace. Off the living room was a small dining area, ideal for my office. I couldn't live without my desk; in fact, that's where I spent most of my non-tub time—munching on snacks, watching the "idiot box" and tinkering with my script.

After the bathroom and the office, the bedroom was extremely important. That was where I'd be spending a lot of time with Simon, if he ever decided to get his ass back into the country…I shook the thought out. *Gotta keep your head in the game, Sylvie, can't dwell on him now!*

With one goal in mind, I sized up the owner—an older gentleman, seemed like the friendly/gentle type, possibly sentimental? I decided to approach cool, calm, and collected, trying to wipe the desperate out of my eyes before shaking hands (I REALLY wanted this place!), and presently made the acquaintance of Milton. Uncle Milty just kept sweetening the pot. The rent? $1,100, unheard of for a one bedroom in West Hollywood. Pet policy? Loved 'em (nice apartments NEVER allowed pets! It had to be a good omen). He'd owned the building for many years. He used to live here with his wife and wanted to make sure he found the right tenant…Oh boy, he was emotionally attached. Turning up the charm while keeping my cool, I let him know I was very interested in renting his lovely apartment.

My heart began sinking when Uncle Milty started describing the lovely married couple who had given him $500 an hour ago to hold the property while he checked their credit, and my stomach was in a free fall by the time he got around to the UCLA student next in line (a "very nice boy" apparently, who was STEALING MY APARTMENT!). My smile felt sticky and fake as he told me I was third in line and he'd give me a call.

Pulling out my last card, I handed him one of the twenty photocopies of my credit report I'd been so proudly carrying around, just in case. He didn't even seem impressed by my perfect credit. I left Milton with an application and little optimism.

Back in my car, I'd already exhausted myself, imagining hitting the pages and the pavement once again if Milton called me with the worst news. I was so burnt-out thinking about it I considered giving up on moving altogether and looking for some other means to satisfy my passion for change. A new boyfriend perhaps?

NO! I had to keep the faith, I would get it! Milton WOULD call and say I got the place. Visualize…in the bathroom…my puppy lying next to me while I read magazine after magazine, eating M&Ms as my skin turns pruney in *my* new colossal bathtub, sleeping with Simon in *my* new bedroom, preparing chips and dip in *my* new kitchen, eating guacamole watching trash TV at *my* desk!

It was all about positive thinking, I reminded myself as I slid the key into my ignition; we get what we think about, so we must dream about what we want. I wholeheartedly believed this, but on the other hand, I'd been anticipating Simon for a few months now, so where the heck was he?

CHAPTER 2

I strolled up to my front door, anticipating Trouble just on the other side…and I couldn't have been happier about it.

True to her name, Trouble was my gorgeous two-month-old Golden Retriever puppy, rescued on the side of the 10 Freeway a month ago. She was peering out of the bushes, freezing and shaking and scared to death, flinching at every car that passed. Thank god she didn't venture into the traffic. I happened to notice her when the jerk in front of me cut me off so aggressively I ended up on the side of the freeway, cussing until the sight of her little head peering out of the shrubbery took my breath away. *Everything happens for a reason.*

She was completely freaked out, but as soon as she saw me getting out of the car, she ran straight into my arms. I loved her instantly.

How could anyone dump a helpless, cute, little puppy on a freeway? Forget cute, forget puppy—how anyone could dump ANY animal, anywhere, was beyond me. People who abuse animals and children are cowards and beyond sick. They're the lowest of low, horrible, wretched human beings and total wimps for picking on a living thing that can't defend itself. Imagining the sicko who dumped my beautiful girl on that busy road made my skin crawl. I loved Trouble more than I could've ever imagined. She was my best bud.

My car visualizations had me back on track, and Trouble and I greeted each other with excited kisses and hugs.

"Guess what I found, sweetheart!" I crooned, petting her soft red fur, "How do you feel about a new home? I don't even have to sneak you in!"

Trouble danced around on her big puppy paws, and I started taking mental stock of our current digs. Moving every year had dissuaded me from ever hoarding things that weren't absolutely precious to me (who wants to move more stuff than they have to?), and having a new puppy in the house meant that no clutter piled up for her to make trouble with. With the exception of some framed family photos, there really weren't too many breakables to consider.

I wandered over to the pictures, running a finger lightly over the frames to check for dust. I wondered about maybe culling down some of these; they aren't all happy thoughts.

First up on the chopping block would be the Balboa Island family home I was born and raised in, which, while lovely in itself (and surrounded by yummy surfer boys!), still made me itchy and anxious. I couldn't wait to get out of uptight Orange County, otherwise known as the "Orange Curtain." I craved some texture in my life and OC wasn't going to provide it. Hollywood was calling my name. LA clubs were my home away from home, and so at the tender age of twenty-one, it seemed logical to get the heck out and move to party-land.

I was now firmly planted in Beachwood Canyon, just below the Hollywood sign. I absolutely loved it here; I had no desire to go back to my roots thirty-five miles down south, even as I bounced around apartments each year.

The next photo I considered putting away was a snapshot of my parents and me taken at my tenth birthday, shortly before they divorced. I had a pretty normal life until my parents told my sister and me they were divorcing. We had no clue it was coming. I don't recall my parents ever fighting, not even once. It was pretty shocking and bizarre.

The situation was off the wall. My sister Florence and I moved in with Dad, while Mom ran off to Europe with her assistant. Talk about role reversal. She had worked in an art gallery part-time and had an assistant. What I couldn't figure out was why she needed an assistant if she was only part-time? Then I had my answer—to bonk and run off with her. She was forty-five and he was twenty-two, so cliché it made me want to puke; although I must say, I had a crush on the guy and had no clue he was getting my mom "off" on a regular basis. She didn't even need the job, she was just bored.

He was hot, a surfer dude with medium blondish locks and a body to die for. What I would have given to see him naked, to touch him… to…ahem, I just mean that guy should have waited a few years and ran off with me, not my mom for god's sake!

My mom was stunning, which in retrospect was probably how she got this guy in the first place. You don't hear too many stories about a forty-five-year-old woman using her great personality to snag a hot twenty-two-year-old. In the photo, she looked ten years younger, dressed pretty hip, cooler than I was, and I thought I was the stylish one.

What these two were going to do in Europe was beyond me, but I'm sure Mom was probably going to try to bleed some more money out of Pops, which she never got a chance to do.

When she left, I never wanted to speak to her again…and I didn't. I couldn't stand to watch what she was doing to poor Pops. I touched his face lightly in the photo and my heart broke a little again, wishing I could have saved him the pain. He was such a wonderful, caring, genuine man. Pops stood about 6'2", and he still had a full head of wavy gray hair. He was always smiling and cracking jokes. I still just didn't get it, how Mom could leave him; he seemed like he'd be such a great partner. It's not like he was a fat, ugly, asshole, but as we all know, no one really knows what goes on behind closed doors.

Maybe he was just too good to her. "Too nice" is bad when we're going through our asshole, bad boy stage, but it's perfect for a husband! Obviously Mom had issues, which had nothing to do with him. Reeked of midlife crisis to me; she was probably bored with her life, looking for excitement, and the sexy assistant was it. Certainly her loss, she gave up the best man in the world.

She tried contacting my sister and me a few times, but we rebuffed any attempts and she quickly gave up. How bloody rude! She wasn't supposed to do that; she should have kept trying until we came around; we were her kids, her flesh and blood. We were allowed to act like children, but she wasn't. I mean, a stunt like that couldn't be forgiven overnight, but she was our mother; wasn't it her responsibility to continue to love us and try to win us back?

Sadly and shockingly enough, she ended up dying before we ever spoke again. She died in a car accident with her lover in Paris when I was sixteen. Not surprising, they drove like maniacs over there. I cried for ages, but I was still so angry with her that it was confusing the hell out of me. I didn't know how or what to feel anymore. I was an emotional mess.

Pops was devastated; he was still totally in love with her, even after what she did to him. Wow, was that true love? Or was it stupidity? Was there a noticeable difference? I hated watching him suffer; I guess that's what took me away from my own pain for a while.

Florence, my sister, seemed to deal with it better than Pops and I did; she blew Mom off and hated her steadily from the day she left. She wanted nothing to do with her anymore and thought her death was what she deserved. She didn't seem to care, which really blew me away. How could someone be so cold-blooded? I still wondered if deep down inside she did feel some sadness and pain.

I looked over at the professional headshot of Florence. Four years older than me, she was very pretty, with large green eyes and rosebud lips and a perfectly symmetrical face that really irritated the hell out of me. Where my head was a tad too large, and my eyes seemed a smidge too close together, everything on her face was exactly where it was supposed to be. Guys fell at her feet, but she didn't seem to care, which probably made her even more attractive to them.

She was determined to be a famous actress—who wasn't in LA? Acting class and bartending took up most of her time. She said she wanted to stay focused and not mess with guys right now, so I was thinking pass a few my way! We didn't hang out much because we ran in different circles; she had her acting buddies and I had my trendy, club-hopping friends.

I chewed on my lip, and smiled at all my pictures, knowing I wouldn't cut a single one from the bunch. *Not every story here is a happy one,* I thought, *but all of them are mine.*

Completing my slow loop around our main living area, I gave a look over my desk. I hadn't a clue what I wanted to do with my life, so I'd been temping until I figured it out. I had a few jobs in the entertainment industry before I started temping, but none of them lasted very long. I kept jumping around, trying to find something I liked enough to stick with that paid decently. Many of my friends knew exactly what they wanted to do; two were already successful talent agents, and a few would do anything to become directors or producers—and I mean anything.

I was impatiently anticipating the day when I woke up and miraculously knew what I wanted to do with my life.

I never had that sort of passion for the industry, so I figured what was the point of dealing with all the bullshit if I didn't even like it? I got fed up with the pathetically low wages and wankers with over-inflated egos. Since I was *only* an assistant, I was the one they would take their crap out on. I was basically a whipping post, and the women bosses were the worst! I was the one doing someone else's shit works while they were busy kissing ass and working their way up the Hollywood ladder. It was fun in the beginning (who wouldn't enjoy going to movie premieres and exclusive parties, and getting backstage passes?), but it quickly lost its luster, and no perks were worth losing my self-respect over.

So I made the jump from the entertainment industry to temp jobs in…the entertainment industry! What the heck was that? I've gotta say, it was way different now because people tended to be nicer to temps, they didn't want to scare them off. Now I had it made, and work was actually fun again. I had so much free time at work, I even started writing a script about temping—pretty amusing stuff. Bottom line, temping was a sweet spot to chill in and wait for some inspiration; it paid more and I got treated with a bit more respect!

CHAPTER 3

I flopped down on my bed and started ruminating over the giant Simon-shaped hole in my life (particularly in my bedroom!) that I had been avoiding all day.

Simon, Simon, Simon. Who was Simon?

He was the man that got my mind off my previous amorous mistake, Josh the Jerk. Simon and I had been off and on for about two years; it had taken him ten months to decide he wanted me to be his girlfriend, and then another four months to say he loved me. I had a sneaking suspicion I was probably so enamored with him because I couldn't totally have him.

He was *still* in Europe working. He was French, or at least his parents were, but they lived here, so I don't know…French-American, whatever. He had the whole mysterious, brooding, spontaneous, and moody French thing down—and really, what girl can resist artistic European charm?

Anyways, he was a lighting technician, touring with bands all over the world. Set up, take down, get on the tour bus, next location, set up, take down, blah, blah, blah, you get the point; he absolutely loved it. It seemed pretty tedious to me, but to each his own. He liked the traveling part, which I totally understood, but I thought it would be the type of job that would be fun in the beginning and totally grueling after a while. He did quite well financially, and got to tour the planet, which worked for him but was pretty annoying for me. It was still new to him, and there were no signs of it getting old anytime soon.

The part I did like was when he was here for extended periods of time. I loved it because we got to chill and really bond. It was weird when he was gone for a long time and then returned; it was like we were two strangers, getting to know each other all over again. That usually went away after a few days, thank god, or we'd probably never be able to pull off this relationship...which, between you and me, wasn't going so well.

It'd been an interesting ride, but we kept working at it. At times he seemed more into me than I was into him, but that was rare; it was usually the other way around. I could never relax.

His lifestyle drove me nuts. Correction: it wasn't his lifestyle, it was his non-committal attitude that made me crazy. One week he adored me, and the next I barely existed. It got old, so I'd broken up with him numerous times, but we always ended up back together. He would pull out all the stops to get me back, and was always so sweet about it. He'd come around to tell me how much he missed me and how sad he was that I wasn't in his life, blah, blah, blah. I ate it up every time, because he seemed totally sincere. I believed he was an honest person, and he wasn't trying to mess with my mind, but he was emotionally immature and selfish.

One of my fatal flaws is that I'm a "fixer," so I wanted to help him get over his confusion. I wanted him to know how much I cared and that I wasn't going to hurt him like his last girlfriend. My mistake, you can't change a man. He was who he was. I knew that now. And no man wanted a mother.

Getting sleepy, I started picturing his physical attributes to avoid the emotional minefields. He had that look that made me weak in the knees: 5'10" with an athletic build; his arms and legs were super-lean and perfectly defined. Nothing was more hideous than a guy who worked out constantly and kept getting bigger and bigger with absolutely no definition. It's like they looked bloated or something and then they walked funny, like they had crap in their pants. I was sure there must be women out there who liked that look, but I'd never met any.

My first boyfriend had a perfect body, but he was convinced he was too skinny, so he constantly worked out and drank these protein shakes to make him bigger. I thought he was so sexy the way he was, but he didn't believe me. Obviously *he* didn't like the way he looked, and couldn't hear me when I told him how hot he was.

He got bigger, much bigger, and I didn't like it, he looked swollen and puffy. I kept telling him I preferred him the other way, but he thought I was just being kind because he still hadn't reached his goal. We broke up not long after he turned into a beefcake—not because of his body, but because of his insecurities, which basically ruined every other aspect of our relationship, along with his physique.

Okay, I got sidetracked; so as I said, Simon had a thin, defined, muscular body. I was a sucker for cheekbones and full lips and this kid had both! His hair was longish and wavy and it occasionally hung in his eyes, which I found totally sexy, especially when we were in the throes of passion. To top it off, he was very charismatic, which is what, I decided as I drifted into sleep, ultimately kept me around through all the bullshit.

CHAPTER 4

I woke up the next morning still stewing. It was a real drag, because Simon missed my birthday on December 14th, and then he didn't come home on Christmas, and now he was a no-show on New Year's Eve. He kept saying he was coming home in a week, but then a week turned into a month...and on and on. He said he had to stay longer because he was searching for his next gig, so instead of coming home, he decided he would go to London and look for work. The excuses kept coming, which lead me to believe something strange was up.

This last time before he left, we were so tight, so bonded, like we'd never been before. It seemed like we had finally cut through all the crap and were moving forward. The intensity between us was insane! Now he'd been gone for two months and a bad feeling was creeping up on me. It'd been over a week since I'd heard from him; this wasn't good, very odd. Generally we spoke every day, or at least every couple of days.

This relationship had me endlessly messed up and puzzled. Usually my relationships were completely different. I didn't date a lot. As a rule, when I ended up going out with someone we ended up together, and generally in that relationship I knew where I stood pretty quickly.

I knew what I liked, I didn't need to date a lot to figure it out. I'd heard stories about women who loved to go on dates even if they had no interest in the guy whatsoever, they saw it as a free meal and a better option than staying home alone. That seemed so sad and pathetic; they were using the poor chap, and *women* complain about being used? What comes around goes around, karma is a bitch! Personally, I'd rather sit home alone, eat onion dip, read a book, or take a bath.

When my last boyfriend (Josh the Jerk) and I went out the first time, we hit it off right away; it went so well that within two weeks he was pressuring me to fall in love with him! Seriously, he started campaigning for my love in the middle of the cheese section of the grocery store.

He was always quite cocky and sure of himself which, I suppose, was part of the attraction, but how ballsy was that? I declined, and kept on walking to the produce section; I needed some ripe avocados, as I was in the mood for guacamole.

I had been with Josh for two years and he was getting on my last nerve when Simon came along. Josh was way too controlling, possessive, jealous, and insecure (all those truly desirable traits we look for in a man), so I was considering an exit.

All it took was one date with Simon and I was completely smitten and infatuated. I'd never felt this way before, and it felt great for a change.

The night I met him at a friend's house, I thought he was nice, but no fireworks…yet. He called me a couple times, but I blew him off because I was still with Josh and didn't want to deal with it. Plus overlapping men didn't seem like a cool thing.

After a huge fight with Josh, I said f-it and met up with Simon. After that, I was completely and totally hooked. I couldn't eat, I couldn't sleep, and I couldn't stop thinking about him. That day sealed the deal.

It all started at a miniature golf course. He was so charming and attentive, always holding my hand or putting his arm around me, even though I was kicking his ass! It's hard to explain, but there was an incredible energy between us I'd never experienced before. When he dropped me off, he gave me a peck on the lips and a long hug. I was a goner! All I could think about was when I would see him again, and that drove me crazy.

When Josh and I had started dating, he would keep pestering me to get together all the time; he didn't give me any room to breathe or figure out if I even liked him! He pushed so hard I just wanted to run. He kept calling all the time, so I would find excuses not to go out with him. Too intense, too quick.

Then one day, out of nowhere, he had done something very wise— he backed off and stopped calling. Smart move on his part, because I suddenly missed him, so I called *him* wanting to go out. Uhhhh, c'mon. I knew better than that, Psychology 101, but I got sucked in. He got what he wanted, and I eventually fell for him.

Well, Simon was pretty smart right off the bat, I guess, depending on which way you looked at it, because a month had passed since our "meeting" and nothing, not a word! I was dying, I mean really? I couldn't figure it out; we had such a great time, what happened? Josh and I were fighting constantly, so I finally just broke it off—LONG overdue, but it was really tough. What made it even harder was not hearing a word from Simon. We connected eventually, but with this new sudden silence, I remembered exactly how bad and insecure I felt at the very beginning. What the heck was going on?

(HAPTER 5

A month after our very first quasi-date, Simon the Slippery Fish had finally called. He'd been in Bali, working (they do have phones there don't they?). That was a sign of how things were going to be with him, but I just didn't realize it at the time.

We started seeing each other, but he wasn't like the others and I was not my usual dating self. I was possessed; I mean, that was obvious after our first date, but I wanted him to call and see him all the time. It never seemed like enough, and frankly it wasn't that much; he was a tough one. I seemed to pass infatuation and go straight to obsession!

I knew it was best NOT to act on my emotions, or I'd definitely push him away. He would certainly run like a mad man in the other direction. I knew I was doing all the right things—not being too available or letting on how much I liked him, but he just wasn't responding the way I wanted him to.

Just when I thought we were making headway, he wouldn't call for a few days and I would find out that I'd been left out of a few important get-togethers with his friends. It became quite obvious that this relationship was not going to be easy. This man I was falling head-over-heels in love with was one tough cookie. At two years into this "seeing each other" thing, this was still going on. Shame on me, the signs were glaring in neon!

The mind screw was when I was with Simon, I felt like I was the most important person in his orbit, but when we were apart, it was as if I didn't exist. That's the part that really threw me.

Once Josh was totally out of the picture, all Simon's crap made Josh look like a saint; funny how that happens. I was thinking about calling Josh but I knew it would be a huge mistake. My head was pretty messed up. I suppose the old bullshit felt better than the new crap. It was confusing, but I had managed to stay away from Josh, thank god! I was not happy with the power Simon had over me; why wasn't he falling immediately head-over-heels in love with me like the others?

They say when people breakup with someone, their next love will most likely be the complete opposite of their ex. BAM! I went from a controlling type A, to a laid-back, creative, guy that marched to his own drum. It was a refreshing change until I realized Simon didn't have a clue how he felt about me, so Josh the Jerk was looking very appealing.

(HAPTER 6

I had met Josh at a club in downtown. He was quite striking, with a square jaw and green droopy eyes, which tended to make him look a bit innocent—total hoax! His blond hair was short and messy most of the time.

I loved his style: Levi's and plain white T-shirts with funky sneakers or boots. I have this disdain of T-shirts with stupid pictures and writing all over them; nothing was sexier than a clean, snug, white T-shirt with a pair of relaxed, low, slung denim.

He was a musician by passion, but worked as a PA on films and commercials to pay the bills; it was pretty lucrative and he loved it.

In the beginning, he treated me like gold; he was always intense, but it manifested itself in a positive way. He fell hard and fast with no mind games…that came later. Wasn't it supposed to be the other way around? Mind games in the beginning, then people move past them?

I wasn't all that into him in the beginning, but I had nothing else going on so I went along with it. I mean, why not, no other hotties were knocking my door down. This was totally against my usual belief that you shouldn't date people you aren't that into, and the whole thing definitely taught me a lesson. Eventually I fell in love with him, but not for the right reasons; I fell in love with him being in love with ME! I was enamored with the idea of us, and his constant fawning over me.

As soon as I fell for him, he started to change; he became a master manipulator/control freak, although the process was slow. It started with an "off" vibe that I couldn't quite put my finger on. When I brought up how I was feeling, he made me think I was nuts.

It started with him finding something wrong with each and every one of my friends. "So-and-so is a slut," or "look at the way she dresses, she seems so superficial"…on and on and on. The comments would come in all shapes and sizes, always unfavorable.

Then every time I would go out with one of my girlfriends, he started having a definite attitude the next day. He wouldn't mention anything, he would just act distant and peculiar. This drove me insane, and I would end up picking a fight. There were two reasons for this:

1. I could at least get a reaction out of him, and

2. It gave me an excuse to distance myself from the situation

I couldn't handle being around him when he was in one of his moods; it was depressing and brought me down to a place I didn't like. If I decided to just leave because I didn't like his vibe, he would be even more of a dick, which I used to my advantage. I knew that by picking a fight, he would most likely end up saying something rude, so I'd have a reason to leave. Now the ball was in his court, he needed to get rid of the funky vibe and kiss my ass; I was off the hook. Wow, and I had the audacity to call him a manipulator?!

This was the beginning of a very sick cycle: Josh got funky, I'd pick a fight and leave, he'd kiss my ass, then dynamic sex, and brief happiness. *Very* brief, I might add—maybe a week or two, if we were lucky. It was dismal; we were totally clueless in the communication department. I tried to talk to him about his issues with my friends, but he wouldn't 'fess up, so I gave up. It wasn't all his doing; I had no patience or communication skills, so together we had no clue. Where we did excel was in the bedroom, and that was our glue. As much as I complained about everything, I was obviously addicted to the sex and constant drama, so on it went…for another challenging year.

The sex was the best! In closets, planes, beaches, golf courses…everywhere and anywhere. It was definitely my sexual awakening, I had no idea it could be so insane! He'd be driving and stealthily slip his fingers into my panties—I was off to the races, BAM!! In seconds! Usually it takes minutes, hours, days…but this man was very talented!

He brought out the vampy, vixen side of me. We discovered all sorts of erotic catalogues, with lots of fascinating toys. He was always surprising me with new goodies and lingerie—rubber was my favorite! When I looked back on photos of some of the outfits I wore for him out in public, I cringe—but hey, it was fun!

His bad behavior worked in his favor; I slowly stopped going out and hanging with my friends. I was burnt out on his weirdness, it just didn't seem worth the fights. Our lives became pretty "hermity"—we saw no one. It was our own little world of eating, talking, fighting, and bonking. I felt like we were in a cult, but no one else was joining. It was just us! He even tried to ostracize me from my family. It got very strange, and I finally started wising up.

Major trouble started when I began to pull away. He got very assholey and mean. The fighting was constant, even more than before! We were now on a new cycle: two good days, the rest awful. But I kept going back for more. I was addicted to him—the intimacy, his Harley, the drama, everything. He was the cult leader, and I was his only follower.

I tried everything to leave; I read books on addiction, took self-help classes, went to therapy twice a week, and started thinking about Simon and how great he seemed, all of it. At last, it worked, and I left.

They say a person must replace one addiction with another, and by the time I was finished with Josh, I was well on my way to Simon. Although I managed to temper the Simon obsession when I was with Josh, now it was full throttle; I couldn't get him out of my head. I knew what I was doing and that I should stop, or at least calm down, but it felt so good—I found my new fix.

CHAPTER 7

So here we were. It was New Year's Eve, I was Simon-less, driving myself insane, and I had absolutely no desire to go out. New Year's is a total set-up, amateur night, the only night people that NEVER go out get crazy. Last year I stayed home and toasted in the New Year with Simon. We had champagne, stimulating conversation, and wondrous sex—that was my kind of New Year's Eve! Plus I hated worrying about driving if I'd had a few, which I knew I would, not to mention all the other drunks out there. All my friends knew Simon was MIA, though, so they were pressuring me to go out.

Uncle Milty called to give me the other piece of news I was dreading, and I was perusing the apartment rentals, again, when the phone rang. It was Lou.

I loved Lou; she was really cool and great fun. She was always up on what was hip and happening, where it was going down and who would be there, blah, blah, blah—you know the type. She was absolutely gorgeous, with the look that runs rampant in LA—long blond hair, flawless complexion, saucer-like blue eyes, and a killer body (all natural, I might add). The only problem with Lou was that she was a bit flighty and self-absorbed. Don't get me wrong, she was a great friend and I adored her, but I knew our friendship's limitations. She was my party pal. She wasn't that friend that I would call for a night of popcorn and chatting by the fireplace. Hanging out without men and alcohol was just not her gig. That would bore her to tears; she had to be out and about, partying all the time. Depth was not her forte.

"This is insane, I've already found out about five parties…this is going to be fantastic…get a load of this one…"

She was like a runaway train.

"…it's a rave in a huge warehouse downtown…the guy spent fifty thousand dollars on it, and they're going to have little cars we can drive around…and a merry-go-round, all sorts of wild stuff but it's $30.00 to get in and…"

I was worn out just listening to her. "Take a breath, geeeez."

"What's your problem? You sound bummed."

"Forget it, I'm just not in the mood, plus I can't afford thirty bucks right now. I'm broke, remember?"

"So what? I'll pay."

"No."

"What's wrong?"

"I'm bummed about Simon, he hasn't even called today, but I'll tell you about it later."

"I'm sorry…See there's another reason to come out with me, I'll cheer you up! Come on, it's New Year's, and I haven't seen you in a while."

"Okay, okay, but what else is going on?"

"Well we're going to the Hard Rock now; they're having a huge gig for English New Year's at 4:00. They do it every year, it's pretty cool. So come on, let's get going! Go get ready, we'll discuss the other options for this evening when we're together."

Geez, she finally took a breath.

"You seem like you're in such a dead mood…oh ya…Simon… OOPS! Gotta go…We'll talk later, Guy is here to get me, see you at 2:00 and don't flake-out!"

I finally got a word in edgewise to tell her that I would see her around 3:00, because I had other stuff to do first—which was a lie, but I was moving realllllyyyyy slow.

"No you can't!" She shouted, "There will be a line about a mile long, we've GOT to get there by 2:00, hurry, leave now, bye."

Click. She hung up. How dare she?!

I realized what a drag I was being. I hadn't wanted to do anything lately except wallow in my self-pity, wondering what to do about Simon.

Fuck it, I'd go. I'd rather stay home and hide out until it was over, but with friends like Lou, that wasn't going to happen. I had no choice, I couldn't escape it, I had to go. I sounded like such an ungrateful pain in the ass—after all, I was lucky to have a pushy friend to get me out of my funk—but it was times like this I just wanted to disappear.

Oh god, what was I going to I wear? I had put on some pounds over the holidays, and I really didn't want anyone to notice. Too many goodies and too much anxiety equaled Bertha Butt. Women could be so ruthless once they noticed a previously sexy, slim woman had put on a few pounds; they loved to talk shit about it. I wouldn't give them the satisfaction. I looked for something sexy and hip that would cover my inflated bum—a challenging task.

Passing by the full-length mirror, I paused to take a critical assessment—5'5" without heels with long, brown hair, and green eyes. I didn't see myself as a super-beauty, but I was certainly far from ugly. People commented that I was pretty but I found it hard to see—self-love issues, I guess. I thought I was odd looking. In this town of flawless, awe inspiring, gorgeous women, I found myself falling quite short. My eyes were too squished together and my olive skin could look very yellow and sallow, which I found repulsive. This "sallow" look was a direct effect of minimal sleep, maximum partying, and a diet consisting of primarily of peanut M&Ms, Oreos, chips, and onion dip. My close friends had told me numerous times that I suffered from a "loss of pigment" every now and then.

I *did* know that I had some pretty damned amazing days when I looked phenomenal, but it wasn't the norm. I caught Trouble's eye in the mirror from her post on my bed, and she wiggled with happiness. Counterbalance to my critical eye—she clearly thought I was something special to look at!

I had it! I would wear my skinny jeans with this funky shirt I had found at a thrift shop last week. The girl said it was from Morocco, it had beautiful beads around the collar and it was this stunning shade of purple. Best of all, it hung perfectly—unique and sexy, killer combo. Topping it off were my thigh high boots. Piss on you, jealous bitches, the chick with the swollen ass was lookin' hot!

I finally left the house at 2:45, moving *very* slowly, with minimal energy. I couldn't shake the lethargic, semi-depressed feeling, which, of course, as much as I tried to ignore it, could be attributed to Simon. Fuck him!

As I pulled up in front of the Hard Rock on La Cienega, I saw the line was wrapped around the fucking block. Damn that Lou, she was right. I should have gotten here earlier. No worries, I would find a way in somehow; I never waited in lines! NEVER!

CHAPTER 8

It took forever, but I found a parking spot three bloody blocks away. I was not thrilled. This was not the kind of crap I wanted to deal with, considering the mood I was in. I walked directly up to the front of the line, which pissed quite a few people off; luckily, I knew the guy at the door. I did some fast talking and got straight in, thank goodness, or I would have said f-it and left.

What a vibe, the place was buzzing.

"Sylvie, what's up?!? I haven't seen you in ages!" screeched Ally.

"Great, really good. Yeah, I've been pretty busy lately."

Blah, blah, blah, the small talk continued. I hated idle chatter with people I didn't care about, unless I was in the mood—which at this point, I wasn't. Most people who knew me would laugh to hear me say this; they seemed to think I was the queen of chitchatting, a true B.S. artist. That was absolutely correct when I was "on form", but today I couldn't get into it; it was hard work.

That being said, it was pretty cool that everyone was there. This would be fun, if I could kick this mood and open my mind a bit; possibly a drink would help. Lance was hopping around like a knuckle-head, as usual, completely snookered.

"Hey…wanna…beer?" He spit out between gulps of his Stella.

"Of course, you know me."

"What kind?"

"Stella works, thanks Lance."

We shot the breeze for a few moments; I got my beer and wandered off to find Trouble #2…Lou.

On my journey looking for her, I ran into everyone I hadn't seen in ages. The "opening of my mind" thing was beginning as I consumed my beer, and then someone offered me tequila shot and another beer—of course I wasn't going to say no! I was actually starting to enjoy myself; amazing what a few drinks can do to change one's attitude.

"How's Simon? What's he up to? When's he coming back to LA?"

Blah, blah, blah. I mean, come on, give me a break, this wasn't really what I wanted to hear right now. Duh! I was his girlfriend, wouldn't you think I was missing him? *Maybe* I didn't want to go there, especially on New Year's Eve! Wise up, people!

Why was it that once someone hooked up, people seemed to panic when the other half was out on their own? Everyone wanted to be in the know, and question why I wasn't with him and where he was, as if we were tied at the hip and couldn't venture out alone. OMG, I felt that more and more as the day wore on. I was saying the same thing over and over again, and getting pretty tired of hearing myself make excuses for why Simon wasn't home yet. Hell, I didn't even know!

"He's still in London working; I'm not sure when he's coming home."

Finally, after an hour of searching for Lou, I found her by the bathroom on her mobile, chatting with this guy she met two months ago on holiday in London. He came to visit immediately after they met, but hadn't been back since. He was still pretty fresh in her heart, and after the stories I heard, she was still pretty moist between the legs about this guy as well!

As I walked up, she yelled my name so loud I was sure she burst the poor guy's eardrums, and took out a few poor souls waiting in line to pee.

"Sylvie! Where have you been? I've been looking everywhere for you! Hold on I'm talking to Grant," she shifted back towards her phone, "Grant, say hello to Sylvie. Remember? You met her last time you were here…"

She handed me the phone. I hated when people did that, what the hell was I supposed to say?

"Hey, hey how are you? Yep, we're having a great time. What's up with you? It's almost New Year's over there, why aren't you out partying? Oh gotcha, so you're throwing the wild party, enjoy and have a Happy New Year! Thanks, I'm sure we will, so when are you coming to visit?…Um…Okay. Gotcha, chat soon. Here's Lou."

Poor Lou, he had said he didn't have a clue when he was coming back, so obviously her hassling him about it wasn't working. Then he proceeded to tell me how hot and sexy I was, and that he'd like to hook up next time he's in LA. YIKES!

What a little shit! How fucking dare he! What the hell kind of nerve was that, telling me he wants to hook up with me? *Hello Mr. Grant, have you noticed my really good friend is totally enamored with you?*

Wow, some men were just too much; now my dilemma was whether to tell Lou or not. Hmmmmm…I thought not, she'd make up some kind of lame reasoning to make it okay; she was totally cockstruck with this guy and she wouldn't see it. Her excuse would be that he was trying to be nice, blah, blah, blah. Not to worry, time would reveal all.

While Lou continued to tell Grant how much she missed him, I stood around watching the *trying too hard* girls, with their tits out and skirts up to their asses, walking to the bathroom, giggling and whispering about all the cute English guys. This crew had a title—'Brit fuckers'—because they loved to be fucked by *these* British guys—not all, just these specific lads.

These guys were everywhere—on the circuit, at every cool club, all the hip bars, and yes, they were totally hot. They dressed impeccably, had cool motorbikes, and turned on the flattery with their thick Cockney accents. They loved these clueless women, because they made their hunt so easy.

I wasn't Brit-bashing by any means, it was just that these boys had pretty awful reputations...they just happened to be English. From what I understood, they were undesirables back home, so they came to Los Angeles with their cool clothes and slick accents, and voila, success!

The women went nuts over them, they couldn't get enough! These cats took advantage of this positive reaction and fucked all over town like rabbits, leaving behind syphilis, herpes, gonorrhea, crabs, and heartbreak. They were total scumbags, but these silly girls just kept going for it. Silly cows.

So the wanker gang was here (looking great, of course), but my friends and I were privy to the inside info, and knew they were bad news. The enlightened, cool chicks kept away from them; of course that made them like us and enjoy the challenge best, because we didn't flirt with them or drool all over their groovy bikes.

So there was this one girl who had been hanging around outside the men's room, peeking in to see if her boyfriend was inside.

She leaned right into my face, slurring, "I think my boyfriend's in there and he's doing coke without me, that little shit-head. I want some more, he should be doing it with me, not by himself or with someone else. I'm coming down already...o-o-r—r-r...WAIT, maybe he's in his car with some chick, turning *her* onto a bump. What do you think? You think he's messin' around on me?? Have you seen him?"

How the hell was I supposed to know? I didn't even know who the heck she was talking about, and to be frank, I couldn't have cared less.

"Yeah, I saw him walk out with the chick in the rubber dress." I couldn't help it; I had to say it.

"That asshole! That fucking slut, I'll kill her, I'll kill him!" She was going ballistic, "She's probably doing all his coke."

She stumbled off in a state, mumbling, "I knew I should have worn MY rubber undies like he asked me to!"

What was it about people being totally ripped and thinking they were your best friend? Women's bathrooms were the worst, they would tell you everything. I had heard all about boyfriends, husbands, sex lives, and affairs. I was loaded up with the whole story in the span of time it took to wash my hands!

Lou had finally hung up with asshole Grant, so we moseyed through the crowd and ran into our bud Donovan. He had been lucky enough to score a table, and we invited ourselves to sit down. This place was getting so packed it was hard to find a place to stand, much less sit, so this was a bonus. We ordered a couple more beers and some fries with blue cheese dressing—my absolute favorite, but not real beneficial for my large buttocks issue. This was perfect; Donovan didn't mind, he was quite fond of us anyway.

Our goodies came, and the fries lasted about two seconds. While we were munching and drinking, Donovan mentioned Rad was at the bar with some excellent (highly overpriced) E. How my mood changed after a few beers and a fun crowd—I was game for anything. I'd trade depression in for this any day!

I looked at Lou with a naughty smile, "Wanna split one?"

She grinned back, squealing, "Let's splurge!"

We found Rad right where Donovan said he'd be—at the bar drinking a lager, with his eyes glued to the tube. I mean, why wouldn't he stay home and watch the game? But I supposed New Year's was one of his biggest sales days, so he needed to be out in the action.

Lou bent over and fixed him with a beguiling smile, "How about a *good-ee* for us, and a good deal?"

A short negotiation with a gruff Rad later (he WAS a sales person, you'd expect something more cordial!), we bought one and stashed it away for the evening activities. I was a wussy, so half was all I wanted to deal with—this was only my second time trying one of these babies. The first time was a total disaster; it was a dud, and made me irritated and bitchy, without any of that loving, touchy, feely vibe everyone told me about.

With four o'clock quickly approaching (midnight in England), the crowd was getting pretty crazy. I was on my fourth beer and feeling quite animated. It was great seeing everyone.

Lou had disappeared somewhere, so I was wandering around on my own, having a great time. I didn't know what it was, but the days I thought I looked like complete shit I got eyed and chatted up like crazy. Then there were times I thought I looked fantastic, but got no attention whatsoever. It was bizarre, because today I was feeling like a porker and not my usual spunky self, but guys were popping up everywhere. Go figure. I guess it goes to show that we're not always the best judge of ourselves; maybe it was karma, the planets, biorhythms, numerology…who the hell knows.

As I was coming around the bar, I got lucky and found a spot to slip in and lean. I liked to be on my feet, reclining against something to check things out—maximum comfort and scope-ability.

Unbelievably, there was *still* a long line outside. I didn't get why people would wait hours just to get in somewhere—who cared how great the party was, nothing was worth waiting that long! At the very least, sneak in, for god's sake.

It was amusing, watching the whole scene go down: the bar bustling with craziness and raucous laughter, while the restaurant tables surrounding the bar were filled with people eating quietly, seemingly oblivious to all the madness. I was sure many of them were tourists; they were probably told the Hard Rock was a cool place to eat, not realizing they were walking into a British New Year's celebration going off at 4:00 in the afternoon. Wouldn't they question why they had to wait in line so long *just* to eat lunch? The expressions on some of their faces were priceless ranging from concerned to almost scared, probably believing the rumors that Los Angeles was a wild and scary place.

Just wait until everyone started jumping around and screaming, "HAPPY NEW YEAR"—at the stroke of 4:00 PM. The out-of-towners were going to absolutely freak, thinking the crowd had totally lost the plot in the middle of the afternoon. Enough said, I loved it here, and we Angelinos were all mad, completely loony.

"Hey, snap out of it."

It was Dylan, another small crush I'd had in my back pocket for a bit. *Okay, YES, I do have a few crushes, I'm allowed as long as they stay that way…right?* He had caught me in full space-out mode.

Dylan was someone that I was seriously considering having a thing with when Simon and I separated a while ago. I was fed up with the hot/cold crap and ready to throw in the towel, but then Simon apologized up, down, and sideways, wanting to make it up to me—and throwing in shocker #1: he wanted to move in together after his next gig. Which he compounded with the BIG reveal, shocker #2: he said he loved me and missed me terribly when he was away! Wow, I was blown away and completely sucked back in; after all, he had NEVER said the "L" word. So much for that hollow lip service—here we were today and I hadn't heard a peep from him in over a week. Back to the warm body right in front of me: Dylan and I had been flirting for quite some time, but always innocently. Dylan wasn't *that* guy, he would never go there.

We'd been friends for a long time, and he'd always been there for me when I've needed to talk (usually about my dysfunctional relationships). He'd heard all the stories, and always gave great advice and a shoulder to cry on; it was nice getting a guy's perspective for a change. Then one day, I realized I was developing a bit of a crush on him.

Dylan wasn't drop-dead gorgeous, but he was still a total cutie, and his personality was awesome. He was about 5'9", with short, blondish-brown hair, except in the front, where it was longer and all conky and wobbly—a very sexy look indeed. He had this quirky smile and super-goofy giggle that was extremely infectious. Once we started cracking up, we couldn't stop. He was such a dork (like me!), but a cool dork. He was a total sweetheart.

"It's a minute to New Year's…oh, what the hell…Happy New Year!!!!"

He leaned over and kissed me! A real kiss at that, he slipped in a bit of tongue and then quickly pulled away! What the heck was that? I couldn't say I didn't enjoy it.

"Sorry, I couldn't wait, I had to kiss you," he apologized.

The actual countdown began.

"FIVE, FOUR, THREE, TWO, ONE!!!!! HAPPY NEW YEAR!!!!!"

People were going ape-shit all over the place; the crowd was insane. Dylan grabbed me again and we were in full swing, arms entwined, spinning around and enjoying a few more smooches. What a great excuse to lose it with someone; it was perfectly acceptable to kiss anyone at New Year's! I was sure a lot of people took advantage of this holiday to lay their lips on someone new, somebody they would never have the nerve to kiss, or someone they'd always had a crush on…bam, nailed it!

"Screw Simon," I muttered to myself.

"What?" croaked Dylan, in between gropes to my neck.

"Another beer would be great," I said, as I pulled away and sorted myself out.

"Yeah, sure, okay, I'll grab a couple," he mumbled, catching his breath while trying to get his physique back in order. I must say, he was sporting quite an impressive bulge, and was having no luck attempting to hide it.

Dylan wasn't gone two seconds before Lou scurried over, shouting over the craziness, "Wow, what was that all about? I thought you were in a bum mood, coulda fooled me! That was one hell of a lip-lock!"

"Seems I'm snapping out of it, baby! We're here to have fun, and I don't *even* want to think about Simon. Where's the E? I might meet up with Dylan later and take my half when I'm with him."

I felt like a kid in a candy store—I would just have fun with whomever I happened to run into. Left it in fate's hands. One thing I was sure of was that I was having a frickin' brilliant time!

"Forget it, Sylvie, that E is mine. Get your own," Lou bitched.

"Excuse me!? Did we not agree to split one? What the hell is your problem anyway? Was Grant a dick on the phone, AGAIN?"

Lou shot me a look and sped off into the crowd, and I moseyed back over to Rad. Lo and behold, he was still sitting at the bar, not budging, watching the game. His eyes did not move from that TV screen. No matter; I worked my charm and got an even better deal this time. Slipping the lovedrug into my pocket, I made my way out into the dance floor. You know how they say that whatever you're doing on New Year's Eve is how you're going to spend your year? Well, if British New Year's was my omen, this year was going to rock.

"Hey, where've you been? I've been searching through this manic mob looking all over for you," Dylan yelled through the rambunctious crowd.

I conveniently ignored the question and asked, "What are you doing later?"

With a pleased look on his face, he told me Brady was having a bash on Ogden. Without missing a beat, he asked, "What are you up to? Why don't you come?"

"Cool, I heard about it too and was thinking about going, so I'll probably see you there."

We hugged goodbye and I wandered off with a teasing grin—gotta leave some mystery, for heaven's sake. I couldn't let him know that I was *definitely* planning on dropping by.

This day was panning out nicely. I had Lou to thank, because if she hadn't pushed me to come, I'd be sitting at home wallowing in my drivel. Time to find her, make sure Grant didn't ruin her day, and thank her for being so pushy.

It was becoming quite apparent that a solid future with Simon was highly unlikely, so I decided I was going to stop looking for a bigger place. My apartment was perfect for Trouble and I; no more moving for a while.

As I was searching for Lou, the crowd started to get on my last nerve, and I couldn't deal with it anymore; people were biffing into me, drinks were spilling, and these people had totally lost the plot, so it was time to go; this was way played-out, and I'd seen a-fuckin'-nuff.

At this point, my thoughts were on to bigger and better things, like tonight's festivities. I looked everywhere for Lou, but no luck—so I asked Rad to let her know I was looking for her, and to call me if he happened to see her. Yeah right, who was I kidding, like he was going to notice anything but that damn TV. Time to get home and ready for phase two, the events of the evening.

(HAPTER 9

That dreaded question again, what was I going to wear? Hadn't I *just* gone through this a few hours ago? It was hard enough trying to figure out how to hide my ass this afternoon, but now I had to figure it out all over again and look sexy! I was feeling extra porky after all the beers and blue cheese fries, so this was going to be tough. Trouble was lying on the bed, watching the pile of clothes grow higher and higher.

Of course! I could wear my tight black dress and throw my funky suede jacket over it for bum coverage. As I was deciding what shoes to wear, I spotted my old Doc Martens.

There was no way I was ever wearing them again, they were so played out. They used to be super-hip and edgy, and you couldn't even buy them here; I had to get mine in London. Now they'd gone totally mainstream, I actually had seen them at Macy's—so sad. Don't get me wrong, I loved Doc Martens; I used to wear them to death, but I liked them when everyone thought they were ugly. I'd wear them with dresses and people would tell me how hideous they looked; that was when it was fun to wear them, not anymore.

As these idle thoughts were bouncing around in my head at a ferocious pace, I filled the tub, adding Mr. Bubble for no bathtub ring. Total relaxation—heater on, tub full, and Trouble curled up on the bathroom floor next to me.

Aaaaahhhhh…the hot water felt so good as I lowered myself all the way up to my neck. This tub was very deep, but it was the typical "too low overflow", which really sucked. No maximum filling capacity. I had to lay wayyyy down to get the water up to my shoulders. Thank god it was super-long, so at least I could stretch out.

I could bathe for hours, and accomplish a lot in the tub: reading, watching TV, snacking, talking on the phone, and occasionally napping. My favorite thing about this bathroom was the old school heater on the wall with the coils that lit up; it was so relaxing, lying in the tub with just the red glow of the heater and total silence.

One of my favorite childhood memories was of lying on my towel in front of this same type of heater, naked, listening to the sound of the water filling the tub and the ceiling fan humming above. I would lie there for hours, reading my library books. Pure bliss. I felt like I was basking in the sun, feeling so secure and happy. Maybe that explains my passion for warm Caribbean locales. Frequently, I would ask Florence to take a bath, just so I could hear the sound of the running water and fan as I was falling asleep.

Besides the low overflow, there was really only one issue with my bathroom oasis—my window looked out at the apartment next door, right into the guy's kitchen. I occasionally caught him spying on me; he would hide behind the curtain and watch me. It was kind of disturbing; he must have known I *knew* he was looking at me, although this probably excited him even more. What was really awkward was that I'd spoken to him many times and he seemed like a pretty nice guy, and he lived there with his girlfriend! I wondered if she knew he was spying on the girl across the way and spanking the monkey?! Creepy, dude!

RIIIIIINNNNGGGGGGGGGGG…OMG, that damn phone, it was so loud that it shook me out of my Zen zone. Uhhhhhhh, I'd better grab it, maybe it was Simon. I jumped out of the bath and ran dripping wet into my bedroom and… *SMACK!* "AHHHHHaaahhhhhh…

shit!" I totally ate it; my right toe thrashed into the door jam.

"FUCK, OUCH…hold on," I yelled at the obnoxious ringing, "HELLO!"

"Hi, hey, are you ready yet? Ogden gets packed, and I want to get there at a decent time."

It was Lou. What a disappointment, I was sure it would be Simon.

"Yeah, I'm almost ready."

"You don't have to sound so happy to hear from me, what's up?"

"I'm sorry; I thought that you might be Simon, and you were quite the bitch this afternoon. You left without telling me."

"I know, I'm really sorry; I had a funky conversation with Grant, and I shouldn't have taken it out on you."

"That's okay, I totally get it. Simon still hasn't called, I can't believe it. Tonight, I'm finally going to say "screw it.""

"What? What do you mean "screw it?" Are you going to hook up with Dylan?" She actually seemed taken aback; wow, she had done way worse, so why would she be shocked about this?

"Lou, I'm feeling completely devastated right now. Yes, screw Simon! He hasn't called or texted for ages, I've reached out so many times, and I just give up. Quite fucking frankly, I'm fed fucking up!" I roared.

Well, so much for that Zen mode; I was now working myself into a frenzy, but it felt incredible getting it out. I was beginning to freeze, standing there wet and naked while Trouble was licking the water off my legs. Great, now I was coated in dog saliva.

I went on a rampage, explaining everything to Lou and she actually listened without saying a word…for once.

"I'm sorry, I didn't realize how upset you were, you always act so cool, like nothing bugs you. I'll be over in an hour. Hang in there. I love you and I promise to make sure you have a good time tonight.

Love you and see you soon."

Lou was genuinely being very sweet and empathetic, which was nice for a change. Usually she was a bit too self-absorbed to notice someone else's pain, although I *had* been telling her about Simon for over a week now…but no biggie.

At this point my bath was pretty much done; I didn't feel like getting in the cold water, and didn't have time anyway.

Oh no, I forgot to shave my legs! Not good, but then again, why did I even need to? It wasn't like I'd be experiencing any heavy action or anything—not my style, even though Simon would deserve it. Then I remembered we were taking the E…what if I…? NO! I was going to be a good girl—besides, the best insurance against any sexual activity was to keep my legs hairy. There it was, solved.

UH! Now my outfit had to change, thick black tights would look goofy with my dress. Light bulb moment! Tight black suede hipsters, sexy low-cut top, not forgetting funky suede jacket to cover up hefty ass. That did it, ready for a wild evening…

CHAPTER 10

Lou arrived on time, and true to Lou-style, hustled me out the door as quickly as possible, all the while repeating, "Ogden gets packed, we've got to get there early or we won't get a place to park... let's go." She didn't even bother to acknowledge Trouble.

Poor girl, she just stared at me with those sad eyes as we left. *Leaving again?* was written all over her face. I was sure the walk I had taken her on wasn't very satisfying; it was basically hurry-up-and-pee, and then I quickly whisked her back inside. I was always feeling guilty that I didn't give her enough attention, but she seemed happy.

First stop, provisions for the evening. I brought my mini-ice chest to keep our backup stash stored nice and cold, because we knew these parties ran out of alcohol and that was not a good thing. Once I got rolling, I couldn't tolerate a drought; preparation was key, and I liked to be equipped for such emergencies.

We got some beer and bubbly to ring in the New Year. We weren't bringing the champagne into the party because once something decent was brought in it was gone in mere moments, and we wouldn't get any! The freeloaders would nab it, because they couldn't afford anything but a six-pack of Schaffer. Anyways, we were magnificently prepared for the evening. I even brought four plastic champagne glasses, just in case we got lucky.

"Oh no, we forgot ice!" screeched Lou.

"Geez, we always seem to forget the bloody obvious, don't we?"

"Don't worry about it; it should keep cool in the ice chest. We'll get some ice from the party. I can't deal with any more stops, let's just get there."

A mixture of anxiety and excitement kicked in as we pulled up and spotted a space right in front. Whooo-hooo! How lucky was that?! I liked getting to parties early to watch the craziness unfold, and Lou liked to beat the rush to ensure optimum parking and no lines. I must say, we were a dynamic partying duo.

Lou already had the door open and was jumping out of the car while I was trying to fit into this damn, miniscule parking spot. It was way too good to be true and I wasn't letting it go.

"Come on let's go, I need a beer NOW," she shouted, already on the curb while I was still maneuvering.

Geez, could she be more impatient?

"Calm the hell down, do you think that maybe I could park first? Take a deep breath, you're really out of control, no one's even here yet anyway."

At this point, I was parking by Braille.

"Damn, this is a tight fit."

No matter, no one was watching anyway…I hoped. It would be nice if Lou could help out a bit, but she'd already cracked one of our beers and was off in her own world.

"Okay, I'm in."

It took me five back-and-forths to squeeze in; I hoped we weren't leaving any time soon.

"Lou, give me a hint why you're so amped to get into the party? You seem pretty darn anxious to get in there. Did something…or SOMEONE…transpire since we last spoke?"

Lou stuttered, something I'd never heard her do before.

"Well…uh…I'm not sure…I don't know."

"Don't give me that crap, I know when you're on the prowl, I can feel the intense vibes emitting from your every pore…c'mon. Who is it? No…wait…I know!"

"What…who…I can't say…"

"Spit it out! Geez! Why won't you tell me? I tell you EVERY-THING."

I couldn't believe she would try to hide this from me.

"I'm not sure; it's just sort of…"

"Get on with it, would ya! Tell me!"

Now I was getting pissed; what the hell was the big deal anyway, and plus I was sick of standing on the lawn in total darkness.

"Oh, screw it, I don't care."

I started walking to the party. I knew if I pretended to not care, she would suddenly be dying to tell me.

"Good, because I'd rather not get into it anyway, it's a little embar-rassing."

Great. Now what? My reverse psychology tactic hadn't worked af-ter all. Now I basically had to either beat it out of her, or try the caring and loving friend approach.

"Lou, what can be so bad that you can't tell me? What's got you in such a tizzy and is *so* embarrassing?"

Lou was looking unusually sheepish, which was actually pretty shocking, and her voice was barely audible.

"It's Matthew…"

"No! No way, Sal's best friend?" I was laughing hysterically. I couldn't stop. I knew it was the wrong thing to do, but I couldn't help it.

"Oh, that's just great, get me to confide in you and then you laugh in my face. Just grand."

At the rate this was all transpiring, we were going to be standing in the front yard for quite some time; the party would be over by the time we finished this conversation.

"What's so damn funny? He's a brilliant guy."

"That's not the point. Matthew lives with that wacko Sal, and I'm just surprised you like Matthew instead of Sal. Matthew is so cool and low key, so *normal*. Not generally your type. That's why I'm cracking up, because I see you with Sal, he seems more up your alley. Matthew is way too laid-back for you!"

"Yeah, I know, but this time I'm avoiding the asshole and going for the nice guy. After talking to Grant today, I realized I'm sick of the same old bullshit; I want something different, and Matthew's been sniffing around lately."

"Good for you. Thank god! I'm so happy for you…and proud. Matthew's a lovely guy."

We looked at each other and burst out laughing as we finally made our way to apartment 203.

Just as I had suspected, it was pretty empty; there were about ten people hanging out. That was fine with me; Lou and I would take over and get things rolling. We had brought in our party provisions, but left the champagne safe in my trunk for later.

As we walked in, we ran into Brady, the official host of the evening. He was super-tall and lanky, with short, reddish-brown hair and sexy green eyes. They were like slits, barely open, but intense and mischievous. In my opinion, he ran the gamut of looking *really* hot one minute and just "so-so" the next, but I was definitely in the minority—most women swooned over the guy.

He was filling up huge Arrowhead water bottles with wine: one red and one white. The wine was along the lines of Gallo, but this party was about quantity, not quality. Plastic cups were placed in a perfect line on his retro red Formica kitchen table, along with chips, salsa, nuts, cheese, crackers, and pâté, the usual Smart and Final/Trader Joe's goodies. In the corner, he had huge trash cans filled with ice and beer. He thought of everyone; for the non-drinkers, he had mineral water, flavored iced tea, and soda. Pretty impressive, he had covered all bases; I mean, this was a major undertaking for him. Usually these parties were pretty generic, without even enough toilet paper to last through the night. Funny, something guys don't seem to think about… but I checked his bathroom, and it looked like he had enough TP for a year.

"Brady, I'm totally impressed, you really went all out on this one."

"Yeah, well, I decided since it's New Year's Eve, I might as well turn it up a notch."

He was looking quite pleased with himself as he placed the full-to-the-brim wine/water bottle on the dispenser—ready for action! I added our beers to the collection, and wandered off to find Lou.

She was scanning the music selection, "Brady, what's the plan?"

"We've got some funk, rap, jazz, house dance stuff, a bit of an eclectic mix, and tons of James Brown boogie material. You know, the grooovin' tunes."

"Whoooo-hoooooo!" Lou was already in full force, moving to absolutely no music at all, "I'm going to have a wiggle tonight, let's get this music going!"

I spotted Emma coming out of the back garden.

"Hey, Emma!"

Emma was one of my best pals. You think Lou was the life of the party? Emma put Lou to shame, she was absolutely nuts. She had this way about her that reeked of charisma and self-confidence. What set her apart was that she was totally genuine (which was a nice contrast to most people in this town) and unlike Lou, she actually listened—what a concept!

She was super-tall and almost too thin. Her brown hair was super-short and she had these enormous blue eyes, and a sharp, angular jawline. If I didn't know any better, I'd think she'd had her lips done but nope, it was all natural, lucky girl. The wonderful thing about her was that she was totally unaffected, and clueless to her charm and beauty.

I was pretty mesmerized by her lips as she walked through the room; this was the look so many women wanted when they stepped in to get their lips done, but they usually ended up looking absolutely wretched, as if they got punched in the mouth or just sucked on a hot tailpipe. Totally bizarre, didn't they look in the mirror?

Emma broke me from my thought digression by tripping over some magazines, practically falling flat on her face while almost knocking a guy over coming around the corner. This little incident was *so Emma*, it was scary. Score! The guy she just about flattened was very easy on the eyes.

Emma stuttered, "Oh, I, uh…I'm so sorry."

Brady came to her rescue. "Jerome, I want you to meet my friends Emma, Sylvie, and Lou."

Lou looked like she was ready to lose her footing too.

"Hi-great-to-meet-you," we all chimed in like dorks.

Lou was flabbergasted and glassy-eyed; she liked this guy. She just stared. Emma looked pretty keen as well. Oh boy, this could get interesting, especially since Jerome seemed to be gazing at Emma and not Lou. But Lou had her sights set on Matthew anyway, or so she said five minutes ago—with Lou, that didn't hold a lot of merit.

Jerome was pretty hot; I was kinda digging him myself (geez, I was out of control!). He was about 6'3"…perfect for Emma since she was so damn tall…lanky and kinda pale, with knockout cheekbones and a beard that totally suited him. He reeked of bad-boy, yet seemed sort of shy—killer combo. Yummy, he was wicked.

All of us were staring with our tongues hanging out, and he politely said hello before Brady whisked him away to meet some other people…but Jerome definitely paused to smile back at Emma before carrying on.

"I'm keeping my eye on that one!" beamed Emma.

"Well, I certainly think he feels the same way about you."

"Come on, let's get a drink," Lou grabbed my hand, and we all went into the kitchen.

"Hey, what's up, anyone up for some red wine?" Tristen, Brady's roommate, was peeking around one of the Arrowhead dispensers, wearing red wine all over his shirt.

"Hey, Tristen, what the hell happen to you and what are you doing down there?"

"Oh fuck it; this damn bottle is leaking all over the place. Cheap piece of shit, screw it, let Brady deal with this—I'm having a brew. I'd like to start enjoying myself at some point!" He sped off, irritated.

Emma was scarfing on pâté and admiring the spread when Brady walked into the kitchen.

"Brady, this is fantastic," she mumbled with her mouth full, "you did a great job pulling this together. I'm proud of you."

She planted a kiss on his cheek as she was chewing, but he didn't seem to mind; he just grinned ear-to-ear.

"Emma, don't forget to thank Tristen, he helped me with all this as well," Brady blushed, as Tristen came back in, on the warpath about the leaky wine. I guessed Brady had a slight crush on Emma, because he was still beaming from his kiss; he wasn't hearing a word Tristen was saying. But then again, who didn't have a crush on Emma?

"Sure, no problem, I'll fix the bottle," Brady told Tristen, still gazing at Emma. Tristen rolled his eyes and walked out.

Lou was watching the scene and stuffing her face, not saying a word. She finally piped up, "Emma, what's the story on Jerome? Are you interested? He's absolutely gorgeous. I have to know…'cause if not…"

"Why are you asking me?" Emma wanted to know.

I had to interject, "Lou, what about Matthew? I just saw him walk in, and he was talking to Jerome—I think they know each other."

I was just curious to see how she'd deal with that one, and then I realized it was a secret; crap, it had just slipped out. Lou's face turned bright red and she said nothing. A quiet Lou was very unusual indeed.

Lou and Emma turned around, looking into the living room to see what Jerome was up to. He was indeed talking to Matthew.

"Wow, I guess they *do* know each other, that is just way too weird," whispered Lou.

Emma finally answered Lou's question. "He's cute, who knows, we'll see what happens. I actually met him last week dancing at Orbit. Speaking of Orbit, that club is losing it fast; I think it's on its last legs, too many 'bridge and tunnel' people hanging out there now. Anyways, he was there with this bimbet wearing white pumps, can you imagine that? Have you ever noticed more blondes wear white pumps than any other hair color? I repeat, kiss of death, white pumps." She paused to take a sip of her beer. "So, I couldn't figure out why this pretty hip guy would be with such an obvious bimbo. I mean she had huge tits and was kind of pretty, but seriously, pink dress and white shoes, so uncool. I figured the situation reeked of sex, nothing more."

Emma paused again to take another sip, then continued, "I'm hanging out with Gidget, and we concocted a plan. I saw them dancing, so I thought, *Let's dance next to them, and somehow I'll get his attention*. I just wasn't quite sure how. We moseyed our way onto the dance floor, and I positioned myself directly behind him and started dancing in my usual, crazy fashion, and accidently elbowed him right in the back, pretty hard. That wasn't even my plan, but hey, it worked! He spun around, pretty pissed off, ready to tell me off, but then saw me and his expression softened. I apologized profusely, explaining what a klutz I am, which is true…he said it's wasn't a big deal, but he kept staring at me like he was in a daze, and she looked pissed."

Emma was cracking up, choking, and trying to whisper all at the same time. She didn't want Jerome to hear. It must have looked like quite a scene in the kitchen, all of us huddled together, laughing hysterically. She pulled herself together and continued.

"She knew exactly what I was up to. Since I got a positive reaction from him, I hung close, talking to Gidget, making intense eye contact with him at frequent intervals. I wanted to make sure he knew that I was interested, and then I walked away. I hung by close enough for him to see me, but I was finished with my part. It was his turn to put in some effort; I wasn't going to make it too easy on him. When I was dancing on the go-go stand with Gidget, I noticed he was watching me intensely while ol' White Shoes was glaring at him, then back at me. Towards the end of the evening he finally came up to me, handed me a beer and well…the rest is history."

"What do you mean the rest is history? You can't keep us hanging like that! What happened to the bimbo?" Lou spouted out.

Emma took another bite of pâté.

"When he came up to me, Gidget disappeared so we could be alone. Basically, it was idle chitchat—names, jobs, blah, blah, blah— and then I asked him who the blonde was, but he skirted the question and asked me what I was doing for New Year's Eve. Now here he is. The funny thing is I didn't even mean to trip over him in the living room, that was a total coincidence; it was just me being my typical clumsy self."

I wanted to know more. "So, you don't know if white pumps is his girlfriend?"

"I haven't a clue, but it's really not that important, at this point anyway. One step at a time…Shhh, here he comes, let's chat later."

Lou and I looked at each other as Emma trailed out of the kitchen with Jerome, smiling; they did look super-cute together.

I threw my beer bottle in the recycling bin and grabbed another one. "Lou, another beer?"

"Sure."

"What's wrong with you? You seem so mellow. That's not like you."

"Just thinking. Matthew's out there, and I'm a bit nervous. I need to let him know I'm interested, and I'm not sure how to do it without being too obvious."

"Umm, Lou, the guy already has a major crush on you, so why not be obvious? Just ask him to go outside and plant one on him; I'm sure he'll be thrilled to stop wondering if you like him as well."

"You think?"

"Duh!"

"Okay, make it two beers, I'm patio-bound."

"Good luck."

Thank god she was off the Jerome kick and back onto Matthew; she was a fickle one, to say the least.

The buzz was building in the living room; the party was finally taking off. Time to join the festivities and see what the heck was going on. My one and only responsibility tonight was to forget about that damned Simon and have fun.

Wow, the living room was packed; it all seemed to happen while we were chatting in the kitchen. Quite a few people I didn't know, and a choice few I wasn't in such a hurry to speak to, so I wandered off to check out the patio.

Out of nowhere, thoughts of Simon crept into my noodle; I felt a wave of sadness and went a bit flat. As much as I tried not to let it bother me, it did. I missed him, I loved him, and I wanted him here with me to celebrate the New Year, damn it!

I was pissed as hell at him for not reaching out; I just wished he'd be more consistent. I knew you couldn't change a man, and this was who he was, but it was tough to swallow. It would be simple if he was a cold fish *all* the time, then I would have no interest in him at all—but no such luck. He waffled back and forth, and that's where the mind screw came in. When he was loving and affectionate, he was unbelievable, but then he went into his cold mode and it was absolutely horrible! He entered into his own little world, totally self-absorbed and distant. Why couldn't there be a middle ground?

Hanging out with Emma always reminded me of Simon, because I met her through him. His best friend Terrance had come over from England to visit, and she was his girlfriend. We hit it off right away, you know that vibe, when you meet someone and you just *know* you'll be great friends. She was living in London at the time, but when she broke up with Terrence, she moved to Los Angeles.

She modeled in London, but that didn't necessarily translate into the LA market; she managed to get an agent right off the bat, and had been working a bit—not tons, but enough to pay the bills and have some fun money. She loved LA, so there was no chance of her going back home anytime soon. Thank god, I'd miss her too much!

I felt a bit of a tickle on my neck and then a soft kiss, as a low voice whispered, "Happy New Year, baby."

I swung around in shock; it was Dylan, standing mere inches from my face! What a savior, thank you universe; I was slowly sinking into Simon sadness, but that got cut short, thanks to Dylan!

(HAPTER II

Dylan and I wandered through the party, chatting with everyone we knew; the place was packed. Everyone we knew was there, pretty much the same people that were at the Hard Rock and many that weren't. The drug boys were there in full-throttle, with their E, coke, and skunky ganja. Taking Rad away from a TV did wonders for his personality, he was actually quite cheerful. I remembered the pill in my pocket—New Year, no regrets!

Dylan pulled me into the kitchen, all giddy and animated. "I'm so excited I ran into you, let's have some champagne!"

He pulled a lovely bottle of Veuve Clicquot from the freezer. "No way, my favorite!"

He didn't say a word; he kept his eyes glued on me as he maneuvered around the kitchen, grabbing glasses from the cabinet and opening the champagne. I was just impressed he didn't trip over anything. The cork blew across the room and ricocheted off the refrigerator, missing my head by mere inches. "WHOAAA…" I ducked just in time.

"Ooops, sorry."

He finally looked away to fill our glasses with that delicious, crisp liquid I loved so much—bubbly euphoria was just around the corner. He handed me my glass, "I'm so happy you're here…cheers."

We toasted and sipped, eyes locked.

Adrenaline kicked in. "Let's check out the scene!" I grabbed his hand and pulled him into the living room, but he suddenly pulled me into the hallway. So much for socializing, but it was a great spot for peeping into the living room, and no one could see us snogging. He wrapped his arms around me; it felt sooooo nice, and before I could catch my breath he was kissing me passionately. So lovely, exactly what I needed. I hadn't kissed anyone else like this since I'd started seeing Simon; I had officially stepped into cheater territory.

His kisses were slow and sensuous, with a serious undertone of lust; my legs started to quiver and a tingle worked its way up my thighs. My conscience started making a ruckus: *get a hold of yourself, you've got a boyfriend!* This was not the time to be arguing with myself; *no, screw Simon, I deserve this, he's an asshole, just shut up and go with it, damn it!*

We were fully entangled when I felt Dylan's cock throbbing against my left thigh. OMG, I was gone, totally on fire, all I wanted to do was slip my hand inside his jeans and fondle him—*NO! What the heck are you thinking, calm down!* I opened my eyes, hoping to jolt myself out of the moment, before I did something I might regret.

I diverted my attention, though our lips were still locked, to what was going on in the living room, bringing myself back down to earth. I was scoping the crowd and my heart stopped; I froze, and all that passion turned to absolute stone. WTF! I couldn't believe my eyes—there in the living room stood fucking SIMON.

*No, it can't be! Simon isn't even in the country, no, this guy just looks like him; it's not him…*before he turned around and *IT'S HIM!* Just to make matters worse, he was not alone, he was with a woman…and even worse again, she was not exactly ugly. Bitch was with my man! That prick! That bitch! My stomach hit the floor, and I pulled away from Dylan in a panic. All the blood had drained from my face.

Oh my god, this was truly a dreadful situation. What should I do? Thank god Simon couldn't see me in the alcove, so I had time to regroup and sort myself out. *Who's the guilty one here?* Simon wasn't making out with Miss Big Bazookas in a corner. Maybe they were just friends, and he came here to surprise me? That would be sweet…now *I* was feeling really guilty.

NOT! So much for that idea. He leaned over, whispered something in her ear and kissed her lightly on the lips. As if that wasn't enough humiliation to witness, she pinched his ass as they walked off. Asshole! I'd kill him. Death was in the air, I could smell it.

"What's up? You look like you've seen a ghost." Dylan looked at me with extreme consternation. It was pretty obvious something was going on, but he couldn't see what I'd witnessed because he was facing the wall. I started shaking uncontrollably. He kept asking me what was wrong, but I couldn't speak. My face was burning hot, and my heart felt like it was going to beat right out of my chest. I was in a total state of shock. Dylan turned around to see what had me in such a state.

"Oh, shit…oh boy. This is bizarre…uh, isn't he supposed to be in Europe somewhere?"

"Yes, this is peculiar," I said, with a heavy dose of sarcasm, "and it certainly doesn't look like he's here looking for me!"

Dylan looked at me like I was the biggest hypocrite ever, which I obviously was.

"Yeah, yeah, don't even say it," was all I could come up with. But this was different, wasn't it? Simon royally fucked me over first, and Dylan was just my diversion to get my mind off the dickhead.

"Alright, listen, just try to pull yourself together; he didn't see us over here, so let's go mingle like nothing's up. Or better yet, why don't you go socialize by yourself, and I'll be floating around if you need me."

As he walked away, he gave me the sweetest smile. *Why am I with such a bastard when someone so lovely is right in front of me?* Once I had a moment, I would have to take the time to analyze that one;

slaughtering Simon was the top priority.

What the hell was Simon doing at *my* friend's party with another woman? Supposedly he was too busy to come home for the holidays, so what the hell was he up to and who was the chick? My anger was growing to a level that was beginning to scare me. It was pretty damn clear what he'd been up to and why none of my communications were being returned.

"Sylvie," Lou came up behind me. She was whispering almost loud enough for the entire room to hear. "Look who's here. What the hell is he doing here? I can't believe this…"

"*You* can't believe this?"

Lou interrupted as usual, "And WHO's the ornament??! I can't even comprehend how he'd have the balls and the stupidity to come here, *especially* with another woman!"

"No-frickin'-kidding, I'm so blown away right now. The last time Simon and I spoke, I told him was going to Nicky's in Orange County for New Year's. Sneaky bastard! He thinks I'm behind the Orange Curtain celebrating, so he came here knowing he'd never run into me!" My voice was trembling.

Lou put her arms around me and gave me a hug. "It's okay, I'm here for you…for moral support, to kick her ass, to kick his ass, anything, just let me know."

"Thank you, I'm pretty sure I'll need it."

Lou got back on her rampage. "I mean, he's so stupid…well, that's a given…but I mean, come on, LA is a pretty small town, people talk, anyone could see those two together and tell you."

"Lou, stop! Obviously he doesn't give a shit."

I took a deep breath to gather my thoughts; it was time to make myself visible.

"Step back and watch Simon shit his pants."

(HAPTER 12

Lou looked a bit dumbstruck, and then started grinning as I walked off in a tizzy. I must have looked pretty fierce, because as I made my way through the party, all heads turned to see where I was going. I was sure it was the fire in my eyes and hurried pace.

I arrived at my target, facing the back of his giant, over-inflated, self-centered head.

"Happy New Year, asshole."

Simon spun around so quickly, I could have sworn I felt a draft. He was totally blown away, disbelief was written all over his face, and he started turning purple. Good, I hoped an excruciating hemorrhoid was forming!

"Uhhhhhh…ohhh…uhhhhhh…I…hey. How are you?…Um I…I was going to call you…but…but I wanted to surprise you…"

The "accessory" let go of his arm, quickly pulling away and turning a different shade of purple. He jumped about a foot away from her, which I could tell pissed her off.

"So, what are you doing here? Weren't you going to Nicky's party?"

Dumb question, showed he was trying to avoid me, and who does he think he is, asking *me* the questions?

"Oh, I get it! You're trying to surprise me by showing up to a party you don't think I'll be at! What are *you* doing here?"

Silence. He was making no attempt to come towards me whatsoever, or even look me straight in the eye.

More questions came to mind, like how long had he been back and *who was he staying with?*

"What the fuck is up, Simon!?"

I was just warming up, ready to lose it.

"And what do you mean what am *I* doing here? I'm the one with all the questions. These guys are my friends, I was invited, and that's what I'm doing here. What the hell are YOU doing here, and who is the tramp?"

Big Tits stepped forward. "Who are you calling a tramp?"

"Ahhh, wow. The slut speaks. You! I'm calling *you* a tramp." I was starting to shout, and the entire room was staring at us. "You, the one rubbing up against MY boyfriend. Wait a second...hold on...you know what? I just got a brilliant idea: take him, he's yours, you can have him. You two deserve each other. I just decided at this precise moment that I don't want this asshole anymore. It's pretty damned obvious he doesn't give a shit about me, so I don't need or want to be part of this situation any longer. He's now ancient history...he's yours. Catcha later, kids. Have a blast...but I'd watch your back, bimbo, he'll fuck you over too." I gave them both my best "fuck you" grin and bailed outta there.

The whole party had witnessed the ugly scene, and everyone was gawking at me as I stormed out of the party, fighting back the tears. The crowd burnt holes through me with their stares, but the best part was I didn't care; I could care less what people thought. I lost it...I knew it...so what?

"Hey, are you alright? I can't believe that fuck-wit. How could he do that to you?"

It was Lou; she ran up behind me, thank god; I needed her right now. We walked up the street so I could have some privacy for the pending total breakdown.

"What a complete cocksucker. I mean I've been so sad missing him, counting the days until he came home, waiting for phone calls, blah, blah, blah, you've heard it a million times. I mean, what am I missing? What's been going on with him? I don't even know who he is anymore. How could he do this and *why* would he do this?"

I was like a runaway train, reeling out of control.

"I have so many questions, so many things I don't get."

The tears started flowing, so I couldn't speak anymore. Lou was so sweet; she just put her arm around me and said nothing. She let me ramble, cry, and ramble some more. As the tears were subsiding, the anger found its way back again.

"Look…I mean…I don't get it. Where the hell is he? Shouldn't he be out here trying to explain what's going on?"

Lou finally spoke. "This is just too strange; did you notice that chick had some sort of an accent?"

The first words out of Lou's mouth certainly weren't making me feel any better. What was that supposed to mean? I knew Lou was just trying to break the silence, but it got me thinking in a direction that made me sick to my stomach.

She continued, "I bet he met her there and she came back with him."

OMG, slide the knife in a little deeper, why don't you? This was killing me, but truth be told, I thought she was right. My mind was spinning; he must have met her in London. Maybe this had been going on for a while…that would certainly explain the non-communication.

"Sylvie, Sylvie!" Lou was trying to get my attention. I looked up too late to act on her warning—he was standing in front of me.

"Sylvie, can we talk?"

Oh my…had he actually decided to explain his contemptible behavior and try to rectify the situation?

"Uh, Sylvie, I think I'll get going back to the party. I'll see you back inside…"

With that, Lou was outta there. We were left alone and it felt way strange, like he was a total stranger. I didn't like it. I didn't like anything about this evening.

"Can't wait to hear this one." I stood there, staring at him with daggers in my eyes, waiting, hoping, for an explanation.

"I'm sorry. I am so sorry; I was going to call you. I just needed some time…some time to think…uh, about…"

"What? Oh please, not that! What did you need time for this time?"

"I don't know…I mean…I needed some time…some time to think about things."

My knees started wobbling, and I felt nauseous. The realization of what he was trying to say killed me: *he wasn't happy with us.* I had many, SO MANY questions, and I certainly wasn't going to make it easy for him. Playing stupid was my game plan, making sure he explained every fucking detail there was to explain, until I was completely question-less.

"Think about things? How cliché! What does that mean? What *things*? A couple months ago, YOU said YOU wanted to move in together, YOU told ME how happy you were. I'm totally fucking confused."

"I know, but then I was…"

I interrupted, "Wait a second, how long have you been back? Where have you been staying? You could have at least called and told me how you were feeling; what are you feeling?"

I was getting more and more agitated, and my voice was getting louder by the moment. The questions were firing out at a ferocious pace, and the stupid thing was that I didn't even give him a chance to answer; after all, answers were what I was looking for, so I should have just shut the f-up and listened, but I was out of control.

"So who the hell is that chick that was hanging all over you in there?"

He didn't answer. I shoved him, and asked again.

"WHO IS SHE? Tell me who she is!"

I needed him to explain, and quickly, because I was rapidly losing the plot.

Silence.

"Please, the truth!"

"I…I…just…" he stuttered, trying to figure out what to say.

I had to interrupt again, didn't I? God, I wished I would just shut up and hear what he had to say…but I couldn't.

"You're such an asshole. Our last dinner before you left, you said that you couldn't wait to come back so we could get a place together. Living together wasn't *my* idea, it was yours. When you mentioned it, I remember thinking that maybe it wasn't such a good thing, but hey! I was open and thought why not? AND you said that you were the happiest you'd been in ages."

I plowed on.

"Where've you been staying?"

Beads of sweat were forming on his brow, and his eyes were scrunched together in obvious pain. Good, I liked knowing he was in distress.

"I know…I meant every word I said that night, it's just that…well… after I left, I started not knowing anymore. I didn't know how I felt about things…about us. I mean, it felt right…but then it didn't, and… I don't know…I'm fucked up, okay! I'm confused about us, and I…I don't know anymore, Sylvie. I don't know how else to explain it."

"Oh, don't worry, I get it. You know you love me when we're together, but as soon as you leave, you don't know anymore. That's scary."

He truly looked distraught. I actually started feeling sorry for him…for about two seconds. Then I got back on track. I couldn't forget my own pain for his; I'd been doing that for way too long already.

"No, it's not like that, I just realized that maybe it was too soon to be moving in together and…I freaked. I didn't know what to tell you, I don't understand it myself."

"But wait, once again, where have you been staying and how long have you been back?"

He stood there, staring blankly ahead, looking like he wanted to shrivel up and disappear. I thought I actually saw tears welling up; if he didn't know how he felt about us, then why did he look so bummed? I didn't recall him being such a great actor, so maybe he did care. Of course he cared, this wasn't about caring, this was about commitment…and evasion!

"Answer the GODDAMNED question!"

He looked at me, on the verge of tears, and looked away again, this time staring at the ground, still no words.

"PLEASE, JUST ANSWER ME, what the hell is wrong with you?" I shook him and screamed again, "ANSWER ME!"

"For…a…um…about…a…a…week."

I went totally numb. I just glared at him; I couldn't say a word for at least a minute, which seemed like an hour. All of a sudden, without warning and certainly against my will, my face softened and tears started flowing at a ferocious pace. I was so blown away and hurt; the tears came straight out of left field.

"Sylvie, I'm so sorry, I didn't want to hurt you, I just couldn't deal…"

"You didn't think this would hurt me? The emails, the texts, the calls you never replied to…It's been ages since I've heard from you. You knew that I had been looking for apartments, homes for US, at

YOUR request—at ANY time, you could have told me to stop, that you were having second thoughts. *That* I could have handled, but it's this deceit that kills me. Thanks for communicating your thoughts to me…uh…like keeping me in the loop, dude. Fuck you! Now you're telling me that you've been in town for a week, hanging out with another chick! No, I'm not hurt! Not one bit, you fuckwit!"

I was in full-fledged crying mode, and he reached over and wiped my nose with his shirtsleeve.

"You've been staying with her?"

His eyes shot straight down to his feet again; he seemed to be burning a hole through his right toe.

"Yes, I've been staying with her."

I spunked right back up again.

"You fucking loser!"

Hysteria kicked in. I raised my hand and slapped him clean across the face, spinning around and booking it out of there. I ran away from him so fast that everything around me was blurring, and the tears weren't helping. I'd never felt so cheated in my life. Things like this happened to other couples, not to us.

I couldn't see or think clearly. The street lamps were balloons of light; trees were blobs of black, and everyone I ran past was a mere shadow without a face. I was crying so hard that I was starting to hyperventilate. I dashed way past the party, and found a porch to sit on. I needed to process everything and pull myself together. I felt like someone had punched me in the stomach, a few times actually. Out of nowhere, I threw up and I couldn't stop. Pretty tragic, I hadn't even had much alcohol and I was barfing in the gutter. What a lovely sight.

I positioned myself strategically, so that I could scope out the party while I was retching. After all, I didn't want to miss any drama that might go down; hopefully I wasn't the main attraction, and there would be other productions to observe. That was doubtful; this was a quite a doozy! Another juicy incident would certainly get my mind off me…yeah right, for about three seconds. It was pretty amazing how I always managed to think clearly even when I was *not* thinking clearly…

"Sweetie, come on, please, let's just try to have a good New Year's Eve. We'll talk about this tomorrow." Simon must have followed me, plowing through the streets like a lunatic. Any bystanders watching this spectacle would have assumed I had popped one too many pills, or had too many shots of tequila. It *was* New Year's Eve, after all! The tears dried up as Simon's ridiculous, totally detached attitude blew me right back into reality.

"Come again? You have no clue, do you? Are you completely psychologically impaired? *Have a good time, sweetie, let's talk tomorrow?* What the fuck are you on? What about talking tonight? Has that even crossed your mind? Partying seems to be your top priority, and of course, you have your lady friend to entertain *tonight.* Fuck you, fuck yourself, and FUCK OFF."

The tears started again as I dashed down the street, back in the other direction; I had this damn block covered. I was definitely burning some serious calories running back and forth, I was willing to bet my bum was shrinking already. This time he was running after me; he caught up and grabbed my jacket, spinning me around.

"You don't even know what the story is with Danielle…"

"Story? I don't NEED the story! I don't need ANY MORE of your stories…but thanks for the name, I'll send you both a belated Christmas card."

I jerked myself away from him and silently power-walked away. Simon was a little boy with no communication skills and no ability to commit.

Yes, he's quite pitiful, but what about me? If I was totally honest, I'd seen the signs from the very beginning, but I had chosen not to acknowledge them. We'd been doing this dance since the day we met. I supposed, in the back of my mind, I had thought that he would eventually fall madly in love with me and change. Pretty sad, I wondered how many women had thought the exact same thing.

Right there and then, I saw the light; this was it, the end of the road. I couldn't take it anymore. Things wouldn't change, people don't change, and he wouldn't come around. He'd probably always be "confused," and I didn't want to deal with it anymore. It was too frustrating and way too painful. Maybe there was a woman out there that could cope with it, but it wasn't me!

The reality hurt and the tears were gushing, but I also felt an odd sense of relief. I was finally done. I assumed he was following me, but when I stopped to sit on the curb Simon had disappeared back into the night.

You think I would've learned, at the end of the day, the guy couldn't be bothered. Oh, he cared all right, but only about himself. It was hard to believe that after two years I was still surprised by his inconsistent behavior. I was sure he'd gone back to the party to find *Danielle*. Bastard.

I knew I told him to fuck off, but he shouldn't have! He was supposed to KEEP running after me, continuing to explain, and apologizing over and over again—he had royally fucked up! Reality was what it was. What a great New Year's Eve, eh? Perched on a curb, somewhere in West Hollywood, I sobbed and sobbed; my body shook so violently it ached. I was purging of all the hurt and frustration that I'd built up for quite some time in my state of denial. Off in the distance, I could hear laughing, singing, and shouts of "Happy New Year!" over and over again. I reached into my pockets, knowing full well there were no tissues to clean up my snotty, tear-streaked face, and felt the dust of the pulverized, forgotten E tablet. It seemed somehow to symbolize how hideous off-script this night had gone. What a great way to start a New Year…

(CHAPTER 13

I woke up on New Year's Day with the worst emotional hangover of my adult life. Totally death warmed over. It had nothing to do with alcohol; when I tallied up my drinks throughout the night, I realized I had managed half a beer and a single sip of Dylan's champagne before the shit hit the fan. The celebratory champagne and "lucky" glasses Lou and I bopped around town to procure were still sitting in my trunk. Hope nothing had shattered…what a night.

As if the universe knew I needed some bright spots, the sun was streaming through the window and Trouble was on the bed licking my face. Her self-appointed job was to make sure I was happy and loved, and she took her career very seriously. I hugged her so tight I thought I might squish her; she truly was my best friend.

The garden looked so vibrant and beautiful. I watched squirrels chasing each other through the trees, while the cat the next door lazed around on the balcony, sunning and cleaning herself. Life really was so extraordinary. Witnessing all the beauty surrounding me lightened my heart a bit, and made me realize just how insignificant my problems were in the scheme of things. I was just a mere blip in the world, and there were people way worse off than I was.

I snuggled Trouble, and felt a bit better…for about a minute, anyways. I couldn't help it…I knew my problems weren't huge in any universal context, but they sure seemed huge to me in the moment, especially as the images of last night crept back into my thoughts and hit me right in the stomach. Yes, I was feeling sorry for myself.

Simon never returned. I sat there, stunned out of my mind, for about a half hour. My future, which had seemed so exciting to look forward to a few short months ago, now seemed pretty depressing. I'd had so many wonderful ideas and fantasies about Simon and me moving to another level, living together. Fantasies, that's all they were.

There was a knock on my door, and I was sure it was Lou. She had already called ten times this morning, but I hadn't picked up; I wasn't in the mood to talk to anyone. Since she was at my door, I couldn't avoid her any longer. Maybe I did need a friend right now.

When I answered the door, I could see myself reflected in her sunglasses—pretty wretched. My eyes were totally swollen, as large as golf balls. Mascara had made its way down to my chin, and my lipstick was totally askew, even the lip liner couldn't keep it where it was supposed to be; I looked like I'd had my makeup done by a super-depressed clown. Obviously, washing my face hadn't been high on my list of priorities last night. Feeling sorry for myself was #1.

She gave me a huge hug.

"Oh sweetie, I'm so sorry…god, I'm SO sorry, is there something I can do? I kept calling you, but you weren't picking up so I just had to come over, hope you don't mind! I think you need a friend right now. That SON OF A BITCH, I still can't believe it!" She cycloned into my apartment, talking a mile a minute. How could she possibly be so energetic after a wild night out? That was Lou for you, always "up" and spunky. I don't think that I'd ever seen her tired and not bouncing off walls.

"Join the club," I mumbled under my breath. "I'll live, but thanks for coming over. There's nothing anyone can really do. What's done is done; he just couldn't deal with it all and decided to bail. Or half bail. Or shack up with another chick while considering his bailing options?

I still don't really get it, but then again, I never really understood him anyway."

"He just left you sitting on the curb?"

"Yeah, but not exactly, I told him to fuck off a few…dozen…times." I actually started to laugh. "But he wasn't supposed to!"

The laughing turned into crying *and* laughing at the same time. It sounded pretty illogical. I seemed to have established a pattern of telling someone to fuck off, and then getting pissed off when they actually did.

"After you and Simon had your scene, he came back into the party, scooped up the bimbo and left. He totally avoided me. What a jerk. Dylan tried to go looking for you, but I told him that you were certainly not in a state to talk, to him or anyone for that matter. He totally understood."

"Yeah, he left a message, but I'm not in the mood."

"No kidding, you didn't even answer *my* calls. Like, I KNEW you were okay, but still, ugh, imagine your last conversation on earth being with that creeper…" She whipped her gigantic Hermès bag onto my desk, and pulled out the Korbel and two of the "lucky" glasses, giving me a wicked smile, "I jimmied your trunk on my way in, never got to toast in the New Year with my best girl!"

I smiled and clinked glasses. "Well, I did talk to one other person last night…when I finally stopped sobbing on the curb, and realized Simon was NOT going to come back, I started driving home with the music BLASTING, in a total daze. The next thing I know, there are red lights flashing behind me. As if the evening could get any worse, I'm getting pulled over! The lights were shining in my rear view mirror, and my eyes were so puffy from crying that I couldn't see a damn thing. The officer came over to the car, and I couldn't even find the volume control for the radio—I mean, the car was SHAKING the bass was so loud! By the time I turned off the music, I was, like, personally angry at the cop, and just start sniping at him about turning off the irritating light. I was clearly not his favorite either, so we were just barking back and forth at each other. He scrutinized my license and registration for like five minutes, and all I can picture is how I'm going to get hauled into jail for looking like some known criminal; I'm like, actively trying to figure out who is most likely to take my one collect call in the middle of the night, from jail, on New Year's." Lou was cracking up; at least someone was laughing today.

"So finally, he tells me I've been swerving, suspicion of drunk driving, etc. I just start unloading on him, about how Simon ruined my night, my life, whatever, about how I had plans to be SUPER-drunk, and not driving, but Simon ruined all of it, and I was completely sober…I could not stop babbling! I would submit to any field test, he must get lied to all the time, blah, blah, blah. He was completely silent, and just marched back to his car at some point, and I'm expecting the worst, you know? Like he's calling in to the station to let them know he pulled someone over on suspicion of DUI, but instead he's got a crazy, and he's going to need major backup…but instead he comes back, hands me my license, and tells me he's sorry I had such an awful evening. I'm just thinking how cool he was, I'm sure he gets a lot of assholes on New Year's Eve, and every day for that matter…so now I'm crying about what a jackass Simon is AND how grateful I am that the cop was chill."

"What a brilliant story, that's hilarious; you were so lucky that you weren't drinking," Lou wiped the laughter tears from her eyes. "Do you want to hear the rest of the evening's dirt?"

"You mean there was something other than Simon and me? Sure, amuse me, please!" I paused…*DON'T ASK!* But like a glutton for punishment, I just had to know. "Wait, did anything else happen with Simon? Did he have his arm around her when they left? Like...did he grab her or anything? Give me all the morbid details, I need to know." Deep breath. I was already devastated, how bad could it be?

Lou didn't say a word for an entire minute, which basically answered my question. "He put his arm around her and kissed her. Pretty passionately."

Pit in my stomach once again, I realized I *could* in fact sink lower than I already had been. This was not good; I had that awful feeling of total and complete loss, a huge void. It was closure I supposed, knowing he was hanging out with this other woman, but I'd been jilted, and that sucked. I tried to think of something positive in the midst of this total depression, but the best I could come up with was eminent weight loss from all this nausea and throwing up. All the stomach acid would probably do awful things to my teeth, though, so even the highlight had a major downside.

Lou jolted me out of my thoughts, "I'm sorry but you asked. I just hope you realize what a jerk he is."

"I think I pretty much figured that one out last night."

My phone rang; I didn't want to answer, but something made me grab it immediately. Deep down, I'm sure I was hoping it was the jerk-off.

"Hey, what happened to you last night? I witnessed the scene, and then you were gone."

"Hey Emma, listen, can I call you right back? Lou's here, and she's filling me in on the dirt that I missed last night."

"No...no...don't...you can't call me back...um...I can't be reached!" She was whispering and giggling; must have been quite the night. "I'm not home. Please, can we talk now?"

"Okay, okay," I covered the receiver and turned around to face Lou, "Hey, Emma needs to speak to me now; can you hang out a bit? I have a funny feeling she's at Jerome's, and I've got to hear this. I'll put her on speaker."

"Okay, but hurry, I've got to go in a sec, I'm getting together with Matthew," she paused and waited for my reaction. "On second thought, I'll just go home and get ready. I'll call you, you should be off with Emma by then. See you later!"

"Hey, thank you for checking up on me."

"No problem, but take a shower or something, you look like hell. Love ya!"

"So, Emma, what's up? Where are you? Jerome's?"

"I'm at Trevor's."

"Trevor's? What's that all about?" Wow, I really *did* miss a lot last night. Trevor was old news, they had dated ages ago. "What happened with Jerome?"

"After you left, Trevor showed up. You know how he keeps calling and trying to get together? Well he parades up to me while I'm talking to Jerome and kisses me, mid-sentence! It didn't sit well with Jerome, I guess, because he walked off. Trevor proceeds to tell me what happened with his now ex-girlfriend and why they called it quits in excruciating detail. I got wind a while ago that they'd been on the skids, so I wasn't surprised. The last straw was when she came home one night, totally wasted, and came after him with a kitchen knife; that wacko had every intention of making him into a woman!"

Emma and I were in hysterics.

"Can you believe it? We all knew she was a loony tune, but this takes the cake. What if he had lost his lovely member because of her? Damn, then the joke would have been on me, what a terrible loss; my heaven's, I forgot how amazing it is!"

"Emma, you went home with him and gave it up already? You slut. You should have made him suffer, for a bit anyways."

"I couldn't, I was way ready, and it's been a while, as you know. I slept with him and I'm damn happy about it. I…wait…shhh…he's coming. Hold on…"

There was a long pause.

"Okay, I'm back. Anyways, that's not the best part; remember how I told you I wanted to cut my hair super-short? I did it! Well…actually no…He did. Trevor cut my hair. Well…not exactly, he…well…um… it's…you're going to die."

She burst into laughter.

"He shaved my head."

"WHAT! No way. Are you serious?"

Nah, she couldn't be, she wouldn't…Although, if anyone *would* do it and *could* pull it off, it was Emma. Her face was so beautiful on its own.

The phone clicked over.

"Hold on, hold on a sec, someone's calling through." I switched over with butterflies in my stomach, still half expecting to hear Simon's voice. "Hello?"

"Hi, it's me, are you off yet?"

"Lou, hold on, Emma's right in the middle…"

"Come on, I've gotta go…" Ugh, that whine!

"Chill, it's hilarious—she shaved her head!"

"What? Ahhhhhhhaaaaaaaa! That is hysterical! Call when you're off."

"Chat in a sec. Bye.

"Sorry Emma, that was Lou, impatient as usual. I seem to forget how the world revolves around her…no, I shouldn't say that, she's a sweetheart; she has a story about last night, with Matthew I guess. Anyways, so what happened? Explain, explain!"

She giggled. "Jerome ended up leaving to go to another party, so I figured bugger him, his loss, so I set my sights on Trevor. I had full intentions of ending up with Jerome for the evening, but *he* blew that one. He probably had to meet ol' white pumps. Who knows."

"Get real, Emma…Trevor walked up and staked his claim right in front of him, and it doesn't sound like you exactly pushed him away. If you didn't run after Jerome, he probably just didn't want to deal with it."

"Yeah, maybe, but if he was really into me, like I thought he was, he would have asked me about it, instead of making an abrupt exit!"

"Yeah, that's true."

"So Trevor and I hung out at the party for a bit and got totally ripped. By the way, I'm sorry about what happened with Simon…"

"Forget that right now, I'd rather hear a funny story."

"So we were already pretty snockered, and then Trevor pulls out some E and we split it. I'm not sure that was such a great idea, I was already pretty gone. The E kicked in around midnight, right before the major festivities began. I swear it was so weird, it felt like a cross between acid and coke, I couldn't stop laughing, and I felt so hyper, my jaw was going nuts and…"

"You mean this was your first time?" I couldn't believe it.

"Yep, first time…we went through the whole Happy New Year's merriment, and then ran out the door, laughing hysterically, and got on his bike and headed to his place. Stupid idea since we were both so toasted…but hey…waddya do…"

"What the hell are you doing getting on a motorcycle wasted? You could've killed yourselves, or someone else!"

"I know, I know, it's stupid, never again!"

"I didn't know he had a bike."

"Yeah, he just got it, an old Indian. It felt amazing, the night buzzing away, the breeze, the lights, the smells…my body felt like velvet, total euphoria."

It sounded so fun…that was the type of night I was expecting but no…UH…

She continued, and I tried to focus and avoid the Simon funk. "When we got to his house, I saw an electric razor on the table, so I asked him if he'd ever cut hair; he said no, so then I wanted to know if he any desire to do so! He said abso-fucking-lutely."

"You're nuts."

"As if this is the first time you've realized this! I picked up the razor, placed it in his hands and told him to go at it. I told him to cut it really short, time for a change…new year, new haircut."

I was listening to this in utter amazement, what balls! It wasn't like Emma's hair was that long in the first place; it was quite a boy cut before, so I knew they were headed for disaster. Thank goodness my friends were such wackjobs, it kept my life pretty damned interesting.

"So the cutting commenced," she started to crack up, "And it kept going…and going…all seemed well, but then I felt a slip and…ohhh boy…lo and behold…I'm hairless! None, nada, zilch! I'm frickin' bald!!"

"Ahahahahahahaha!" I squealed. "I can't believe it, I thought you were joking. Are you serious? No, no way."

"Yep! I'm not joking, I'm bald!"

I was blown away. "How does it look? Does it look good? Does Trevor like it, do you like it?" I was firing questions at her a mile a minute. "Actually, I bet you look fantastic bald. You definitely have the face for it."

"Thanks, yes, yes, and yes! I really like it but it feels so odd! No need for shampoo anymore!"

We were both in hysterics; I couldn't wait to see her shiny head.

The phone clicked; another call was coming in.

"Hold on, Emma. I bet it's Lou again."

I clicked over, "Lou, hold on a sec, I'm still on with Emma..."

"Hey...what's up?"

Oh my god, it was Simon. My gut fell to the floor. At least I had a few moments, laughing with Emma, forgetting about everything.

I managed to keep my cool.

"Uh...hey...let me call you back, I'm on with Emma. What number shall I call you back on?"

"That's okay; I'll call *you* back in ten minutes."

"Make it fifteen." I hung up. Damn, the number was private. I was sure he was calling from that bitch's house.

"Guess who *that* was?" I moaned as I got back on with Emma.

"No! Not Simon."

"Yep."

"Do you want to take it?"

"Nope, he can call back. I can't deal with this right now; I'm already drained; it's a fresh new year, aren't we supposed to feel positive, fresh and happy?"

"Don't worry about it, keep your ground and listen to your gut. He's been a total asshole; Lou filled me in on some of it last night, so I've got the gist of the situation. He's not worth it, move on."

"Yeah, but look where your gut got you...bald!" Well, at least I can still laugh!

"You're right, you got me there! Okay, I've got to go; Trevor and I are heading to the beach for lunch. I'm sure I'll shock a few people with my white, bald head. Hang in there, and don't let him bullshit you. I love you, call me later. Bye, bye, don't be bummed. Now you can move on and find a guy that adores and appreciates you."

"Thank you sweetie, have a blast and keep your head warm."

"Sure, Mom. See ya!"

Well, her new year was certainly starting out exciting, and Lou seemed to be having a good one as well. It was time to ditch my pity party, and start looking at the end of Simon and the start of the new year in a positive way.

I returned Lou's call, but she didn't pick up, so I left her a message. I told her Simon called; that would get her going. I took Trouble out and got back into bed. She sat right on my chest and we both gazed out the window, admiring the gorgeous day. A squirrel was jumping from one tree to the other, chasing his buddy around and driving Trouble nuts. Eventually she grew tired of watching the shenanigans and we both fell into a deep, blissful, sleep.

CHAPTER 14

I slept for about two hours, and woke up with a start when I realized the bloody bastard hadn't called back. Fifteen minutes my ass; he probably couldn't get away from *her* long enough to call. Trouble distracted me, just being so adorable; she was still asleep, with her head resting on my stomach. I looked around my room and noticed the beautiful dried roses hanging on my wall. Simon had given them to me before he left; it was the only time he had ever given me roses. I loved them.

It was the real shits when my boyfriend had been out of the country for over a month and when he finally returned on Valentine's Day, he was empty handed! No card, nothing! If he hadn't realized it was Valentine's Day, being away and all, that would have been fine…but that wasn't the case.

When I realized he was returning on that special day, I dropped a few subtle hints and expressed how exciting and apropos it was. I mentioned I wanted to take him to dinner to celebrate Valentine's Day and his homecoming.

Suffice it to say we never went to dinner; we got into it right off the bat. He informed me that Valentine's Day was a concept the marketing world made up to make large amounts of money; he didn't believe in it and he wouldn't feed into it. I told him I loved Valentine's Day, so maybe he could just indulge me and we could have a nice time. He repeated his inane quasi-political argument again before leaving, and I spent the rest of V Day in bed, alone.

My neighbor Rebecca's boyfriend (a complete jerk, who screwed around on her constantly) got her diamond earrings and took her out to a nice dinner. Well, okay, not the best example, since that one really did illustrate Simon's point about the hypocrisy of the holiday…but still…

The more I contemplated our relationship, the more agitated I got…with myself! Seriously, what kind of an idiot was I to put up with this kind of crap? This new year needed to start with me getting my head in order and moving on. I was obviously de-valuing myself and creating a bad pattern.

For the longest time I had thought it was me, that I was the problem. Like if I did this a little different, or that a little different, he would realize just how great I was and stop being confused about us. I had put it all on me. It seemed like I was always putting myself out for him, giving him little gifts, letters, cards…and not getting much in return. When I told him I felt a bit neglected, he would come up with some pathetic excuse, like, "Well that's just the way I am." I assumed he must have been hurt in the past and needed time to come around and trust again. What a crock of shit. I was so ashamed of myself as I looked back on what a fool I'd been.

Some of our fights had got pretty gnarly, and I wasn't too proud of a few performances. All was well when *he* was in the mood to be loving, but when he turned to Mr. Cold, that's when all hell would break loose. I tried to talk to him, but he would shut down and retreat into his cave, no communication for days.

The resentment would build and build until eventually I would resort to unhealthy antics…which included but wasn't limited to: freaking out, acting out, or just plain losing it. Pouring beer over Simon's head in public places, throwing his clothes off the balcony (his underwear got stuck in a tree for a few months, until a storm shook them loose), chucking treasured items, aiming large dense fruit at the small of his back or buttocks…and, last but certainly not least, driving my car at him full throttle, veering away at the last second. I would have never actually hit him, I just felt I needed to scare the shit out of him. Simon had been bringing out the worst in me, and I was turning into someone I didn't want to be, but I still hadn't left, and that's what was really disturbing.

Thank god this madness was coming to an end.

(HAPTER 15

Lightning bolt moment; my relationships definitely took a turn for the worse when I moved to LA.

As everyone seems to do when they come to this town, I started going to acting class. I sat between Sean and Lou. Lou and I hit it off right away, and we would make fun of everyone who got up to do their scenes. Not a cool thing to do, especially since we both sucked, but acting just wasn't our scene.

In class, Sean acted like he couldn't stand me, but one night we had to do a scene together; as usual, I was terrible and he was quite impressive. When our scene was finished, he gave me a red rose and a huge smile...and then proceeded to ignore me the rest of the class. He wouldn't even look at me! Completely thrown, I became intrigued.

After class, he cut my car off with his topless red MG, giving me the follow-me wave. This guy was way too much, and pedal to the metal, like a magnetic force...I was going to follow that dick and give him a piece of my mind!

He pulled into the parking lot in front of Yum Yum Donuts on Melrose and La Brea. I parked next to him, but he jumped out of his car and went in to get something, not even acknowledging me. I already felt like an idiot, so I started my car to get the heck out of there. He made a mad dash out the door, practically spilling his coffee all over himself.

"Hey, where are you going?"

"I'm leaving."

"Why? You just got here."

"Well, you were taking your sweet time getting coffee, and I had time to try to figure out why I even followed you in the first place."

"So what did you come up with?"

"Probably to tell you you're arrogant, and wayyy too full of yourself."

He just looked at me, completely silent. I was beginning to feel really uncomfortable; my armpits were dampening and my face was getting hot. It was obvious he was enjoying my uneasiness, so I had to say something.

"What did you want anyway?"

"You're kind of interesting in class, a little uptight but pretty cool. I wanted to get to know you and talk to you about your acting…it could use some work," he paused, "Why are you so awkward and unsure of yourself?"

My mouth dropped. What an ass. I started to roll up my window, muttering, "I don't need this…"

He stuck his hand in the window to stop me. Frankly, I was so pissed off and embarrassed, I thought about letting the window smash his fingers.

He leaned in to say, "All I meant was I can't figure out why you're so self-conscious, because you're very beautiful."

What a line. This guy was smooth.

He pulled my door open and crouched down, so we were eye level. "Hey, I'm really sorry, I didn't mean to insult or embarrass you; it's just that sometimes you act like such a hard-ass in class, and I wanted to get a reaction out of you."

Hmmm, maybe he wasn't so bad after all; it was not the first time I'd been called a hard-ass, and he did have lovely eyes.

Next thing I knew, he was opening my car door and pulling me out! So damn pushy, but I kinda liked it.

"Let's take a ride up Mulholland; it's a beautiful evening, the view will be amazing."

I sat back in my car.

"I can't, I've got to work early tomorrow. Maybe another time."

He was still holding on to my arm, "Hey, I really didn't mean to insult you; I'd just like to have a chat and get to know you. I promise I'll get you back early."

I really wanted to go, but didn't want to look like a pushover. He was pretty slick, and I was sure his moves worked on women all the time. I had to be different. Can't go, have to play hard to get, I can't...I can't...I won't...

"Okay, but not for very long."

I couldn't believe I had just said yes! Well, I *wanted* to go, damn it; screw the games and take a bloody risk, for god's sake!

We sailed up Laurel Canyon on our way to Mulholland; it was such an amazing evening, super-clear and warm. It had been ages since I'd been with anyone, so I was buzzing with anticipation as we flew through the hills.

It was such an adrenaline rush, screeching around the curves with the wind in my face. His driving was making me a little nervous, but that just added to the thrill. A few times I thought we were going off the side of the cliff; yikes, he was nuts!

I started freaking a bit because I couldn't find my seatbelt. I'd been searching since we left, but I finally gave up. I didn't want to look like a dork or make a scene.

He pulled off the road into an open area with a spectacular view; it was utterly breathtaking. I couldn't believe all the twinkling city lights, I was completely blown away. He came around to open my door and grabbed my hand, pulling me into him and going straight for the goods!

I turned my head and shimmied away. I wasn't ready to dive right in and start making out. Give me a few minutes, for heaven's sake—didn't he want to get to know me? All of a sudden it dawned on me—this guy could be a total psycho. What was I thinking? I could be raped and murdered, left in the brush. My car would be found at Yum Yum Donuts, but I would be gone. Would I ever be found? There are many corpses dumped up here that are never located. Or would it be the proverbial morning jogger that found me dead by the side of the road? My poor family, just because I needed some excitement in my life, I came up here with an alluring stranger...

He was a man of few words; he hadn't said a thing since his apology in the parking lot. So there we were, admiring the view in total silence. This was starting to feel really weird. He walked a few steps away, but then came back towards me. My heart was ready to beat out of my chest as he backed me slowly towards the car and laid me down on the hood, kissing me.

This was HOT! The guy couldn't make conversation, but he knew how to do something special with that mouth. His MG was getting a good hood buffing, and he started fumbling around and lifting my dress; I realized he had unzipped his pants when I felt his penis against my leg! I freaked, and reality kicked in.

I contorted my body so that I could maneuver away from him.

"Hey, what's wrong? What are you doing?"

"I could have sworn that you said you wanted to get to know me, not "do me" on the hood of your car, or maybe that's exactly what you meant by *getting to know me*!"

Of course that's what he had meant. I was so naïve. He just glared at me. At this point I was convinced he was a real weirdo, and I wanted to get the hell outta there.

"Can we go? I've got to get up early." I hopped into the car, still trying to figure out the odds of getting down the hill without being, like, dismembered. He kept staring me down for a few long minutes, but eventually heaved himself into the car, and tore off down the hill like a maniac. He dropped me off at my car and sped off…I was so lucky he didn't leave me up there. Since I sucked anyways, I quit acting class and never saw him again. Really, it had set the tone for all my future LA relationships—the rules were different here, and if I wasn't careful, things could get dangerous and/or stupid, fast.

The phone ringing shocked me back to reality.

CHAPTER 16

It was Simon.

"Are you okay?"

"No, did you think I would be? A little sleep would magically fix what you did to me?"

"Well, um, I don't know. Can we get together? You know I hate talking on the phone."

"What's to discuss? You said it all last night."

"No, Sylvie, it's not that black or white; we've got to talk. C'mon, let's meet at El Coyote."

Oh great, our favorite place. I was weakening. I really did want to see him, and was still seriously hoping that last night had only been a bad dream. If nothing else, we did need to finish our conversation and put closure on our relationship.

"Alright, give me a couple hours; I'll see you there at 3:00." Boy, was I weak. I hung up, immediately angry with myself, but I had to see him.

I looked like shit; my eyelids were huge and puffy and felt like poached eggs. I would have liked to look damn good, so he would know what he'd be missing, but no such luck.

I got out of bed, turned on some spunky music and hopped straight into the tub. The phone rang again as I was rushing around to get ready, and I raced into the bedroom to answer it, knocking over a plant and tripping over Trouble.

"Lou, I can't talk now, I'm going to meet Simon."

"What? Just a few hours ago you wanted him out of your life and now you're going to meet him? I can't…"

"Lou, I know, it was hard enough for me to decide to go or not, so please understand. He wants to talk, and frankly I'm curious to see what he has to say. I've got to go."

"Oh thanks, earlier you couldn't talk because of Emma and now you're off with Simon. You'll be with him all night, so when will I get to tell you about last night and Matthew?"

She kept chattering, "You don't even care what happened to me last night, you just…"

"Come on Lou, I'm sorry. You know I care and love you, it's bad timing, I'm completely freaked out right now, and I know I'm being self-indulgent, but bear with me, I have to do this. Please understand, I promise we'll talk tonight or tomorrow."

"I won't be in tonight."

"Okay, can we go to breakfast tomorrow? Kings Road, I'll treat."

"Alright, let's meet at 10:30. Please don't let him bullshit you, stand your ground. There are other guys out there, Dylan's nuts over you and…"

"I've gotta run, we'll talk later, see you tomorrow."

I left wearing baggy vintage Levi's, a Vivian Westwood corset, and wedges. Trouble had a pig's hoof to keep her occupied and ensure the legs on my coffee table would still be there when I got home.

I pulled in late but whatever, he could wait. I found him at the bar chatting, and when he saw me, a huge smile spread across his goddamn beautiful face. I was melting; when he turned it on, I was a goner. Pathetic, I had to be strong.

He planted a lovely kiss on my lips.

"Hi sweetie, you look beautiful."

I pulled away. No kissing, please no kissing.

"Thanks."

He stood there smiling, gazing into my eyes, not saying a word, and then he pulled me close and hugged me so tight I literally stopped breathing. What a mind screw, last night he was totally cold and now this. Hot, cold, hot, cold...as we pulled apart, I noticed he had tears in his eyes.

We ordered margaritas, two doubles on the rocks with salt, and hung out in the bar until we were seated at our favorite booth in the Pink Room. Why they called it the Pink Room was beyond me; it wasn't even pink, it was yellow. I had asked, but no one seemed to have a clue. It was the coolest room in the place; it was where all the action went down. The patio was pretty fun too, but I wanted to be in the dark and feel cozy.

I slid into the booth and Simon sat across from me. He grabbed my hands and held them, staring into my eyes for what seemed like forever—probably trying to figure out what the hell to say.

"Would you like to order now?" Billy, our favorite waiter, had broken the reverie.

"Hey, how are you doing? Happy New Year! It's great to see you. We'll have chips and salsa, thanks," Simon was talking way too fast.

Forget this softy act; holding my hands, gazing into my soul, whatever. Let's get to it. Once Billy left, I let go of his hands and jumped into my line of questioning.

"So, why didn't you tell me you were back?"

"I tried to explain that to you last night, I...I just sort of, I don't know, I guess I got freaked out. I started questioning what I was doing—should I live in LA or in Europe, should we move in together? What about my career? Us? Everything? I was confused."

"So you dealt with your confusion by sneaking back into town with another woman? I don't understand that logic."

"No, I just wanted some time to myself to think about everything. I was going to call you once I figured it all out, but then I ran into you at the party."

I was trying to sit quietly and listen. I was curious and wanted to hear what he had to say. After all, I'd obviously been confused as well. Kissing Dylan in a hallway for god's sake! But at least I wasn't staying and probably sleeping with someone else. I didn't want to pounce right back into the fight, but his excuse was such utter bullshit—I couldn't help it.

"But you weren't alone. You were with the other woman you're seeing."

"Where do you get that I'm seeing her? You're jumping to conclusions about things you know nothing about."

"Listen, if it quacks like a duck, walks like a duck, and looks like a duck, than it's a fucking duck." I took a deep breath, remembering my own transgressions the night before. "Okay, so if you aren't seeing her, what's the story? I haven't heard from you in ages and then I run into you at a party to find out you're living with another woman; you had your arm around her and you kissed her. That looks pretty suspicious don't you think? What BRILLIANT CLUE am I missing?"

Billy brought the chips and salsa and quickly walked away; he sensed tension and didn't want to interrupt. I sat back and munched on chips, waiting for Simon to explain.

"Fair enough, I know, it's a little confusing…"

Simon took a sip of his margarita, staring off into space, saying nothing. He was obviously having a hard time coming up with something, since he had been caught red-handed.

Billy had noticed the false tranquility, and he decided to take advantage and see if we were ready for food.

"Are you ready to order? Should I just bring you your usual?"

"Thanks Billy, not yet, but could we have some blue cheese dressing for the chips, please?"

"Sure, I'll bring it right over and...you both look like you could use another double...this time on me!"

"HA! You're right! Thank you!"

He made his way out of the war zone. Simon looked up slowly, seemingly oblivious to the interaction that had just taken place.

"Sylvie, I don't know how to make you understand this, but...Danielle and I have been friends for a long time. We hung out a lot while I was in London. She was coming back over here to stay with friends, so I decided to book my flight with her. I was going to call you, but then I had a complete panic attack. The reality of us moving in together completely freaked me out. I don't know...ummm...I don't know."

"Here you go, blue cheese dressing, two doubles and the guacamole is on me as well, enjoy."

"Thanks!" Billy walked off.

The more Simon spoke, the faster I started inhaling chips. I was munching with a nervous vengeance; I couldn't help but notice that Simon hadn't touched a single one.

"So, I came back and stayed with Danielle's friend in Los Feliz...I haven't slept with her, we're only friends. She doesn't know many people in LA, so I decided to take her out on New Year's."

I took a break from pumping chips and interrupted.

"But didn't you even consider that you might run into me? And you *did* have your arm around her AND you kissed her...or do you fondle all your friends? Why did you want to spend New Year's Eve with her and not me?"

"It didn't mean anything when I had my arm around her; I was just leading her out the door. Geez, I guess your friends *did* report back to you."

"Simon, *I* saw you kiss her at the party and, yes, they told me you kissed her again as you were leaving." His story was such a load of shit. If a friend had told me that her boyfriend came up with this crap, I would have definitely called him a liar. I knew what I had seen; he had kissed her when I was in the hallway with Dylan, and Lou wouldn't lie. I was speechless.

Simon got up and slid in next to me. He wrapped his arms around me and wouldn't let go.

"God, I'm so sorry, I…I really don't know what to say…I completely fucked up. I just didn't know if I was doing the right thing by moving in with you. Like I said, I freaked and wanted to run away. I just needed to chill, but when I saw you last night, and we had that scene, I realized how much I really miss you."

The anger was building…

"So you figured this all out at my expense? You had to fuck *me* over to realize that YOU fucked up?" My voice was getting a little too loud and I was babbling on as Simon put his fingers on my lips and wiped my tears with his napkin.

"Please…I'm so sorry, can we try to start over and go back to where we were before I left? I'm sure now that I want us to live together. I really care for you."

I really care for you?

"You really care for me? How about 'I really love you'?"

"Yes, I do Sylvie, I love you."

"I don't know how I can ever believe you. What if you pull this maneuver next week, next month, or next year? What about Danielle? I saw you kiss her, and you've pulled this kind of crap before; once things get too good, you freak out and run."

I couldn't see; the tears were flowing and the golf-ball eyelids were settling back in. How dreadful I must have looked, with snot dripping out of my nose and a blotchy red face. Billy kept circling our table, attempting to take our order and then deciding against it for obvious reasons.

"Let's try, let's think positive, come on sweetie," Simon whispered, kissing my eyelids.

Positive was not even close to what I was feeling, but I was melting as he kissed me. He was saying and doing everything I wanted him to do last night. I gave into it, knowing full well I was being a fool, but I was in dire need for love and it felt so good to be back in his arms. We had both screwed up, but maybe we could build a stronger relationship now.

The rest of the evening we carried on like a couple of lovebirds. The tears stopped, but my eyes were still swollen; thank god it was dark in El Coyote. As usual, I unscrewed the light bulb above our table to make it even cozier. Billy was finally able to take our order and by this time we'd consumed three doubles, so we were truly off our faces. I kept getting stabs of reality; I knew what I was doing was wrong, but I had lost all sense of logic, and all I cared about was bandaging the wound Simon created and feeling his love. I wanted so badly to believe him; I wanted to trust that we could be together, once and for all, but my gut was screaming at me to tell him to go to hell and walk out.

That inner voice was silenced when his hand disappeared under the table and slid between my legs.

His finger fluttered lightly back and forth over my Levi's, creating an unbelievable vibrating sensation. The warmth of the low lights, Simon's fondling, and the margaritas had put me in a lovely, horny daze as I started to squirm. I arched under the table to get him to push harder...faster...I looked at him and he was staring at me intensely. I started kissing him as I reached under the table to feel how aroused he was…he was totally busting through his jeans. I stroked him and grabbed his hand, pushing it harder into me. I was so close to exploding, just trying to stay composed—we were in the middle of the Pink Room, for heaven's sake! It was such a turn on, because no one could tell what was going on; well, maybe they could. No, if they *really* looked at me, they'd just think I was a lush having an asthma attack.

Simon slowly unzipped my jeans, sliding his fingers into my panties. He teased me, circling around and around, and then pushing deep inside me which…"Oh my god, Simon…"

I was trembling and squirming all over that damn booth, and I held onto him for dear life. I was trying to be quiet and muffle my moans on Simon's neck, but I noticed Billy walk by with a huge grin on his face. OMG, this was certainly a first; I had come at El Coyote in a Naugahyde booth!

We melted into each other as we sat kissing and giggling, wallowing in the loveliness of it all. We had one more margarita while we cuddled, not saying much of anything except how great it felt being together again; it had been way too long.

CHAPTER 17

As soon as I opened the door, Trouble went absolutely nuts, spinning in circles, chasing her tail. She seemed a little suspicious of Simon at first, but she quickly calculated I was pretty keen on this guy so she warmed up to him. I had told him on the way home that I didn't want to get a new apartment; if he wanted to live together, it would be here, with me. I became hyper-aware, wondering what he might be thinking; would he like my place, for the both of us to live? I felt like he was seeing it for the first time.

In a weird way, I felt like I was seeing it for the first time too, at least in this context.

Why had I even been looking for another place? I supposed I had thought my apartment wasn't big enough for both of us, or maybe I was just driven by my need for change. I was only paying $1,050, which was a smokin' deal, so why move? Plus, with our relationship volatility, I didn't want to get stuck with rent I couldn't afford. I took a moment to admire the floor-to-ceiling French windows that made my smallish living room seem much larger, and the small fireplace and hardwood floors that made it seem so cozy. I was shopping my own apartment, and I liked it.

Simon still hadn't said a word. He was walking around looking at everything, totally silent. I was getting nervous; what if he didn't want to live here? We walked into the kitchen, typical old style with lots of tile and French windows. I was looking at everything with new eyes, wondering what he was thinking.

He made his way into the bedroom—smallish, with floor-to-ceiling French windows looking out to the garden. I admired my bed, an antique I got at Wertz Brothers ages ago. I was going for the cozy, sensuous vibe, with a super-puffy feather comforter and fabric I had hung from the ceiling, draping around the sides of the headboard to create a canopy effect. Very comfy.

Finally...the man said, "This is perfect for both of us! Let's do it!"

With that, he grabbed me and threw me onto the bed. Trouble was getting jealous, trying to get our attention while we were making out and rolling around on my bed—no, OUR bed.

Uh-oh—Trouble needed to pee.

"I have to take Trouble out."

He kept kissing me, practically tearing our clothes off. I struggled to get up, but he pushed me back down, licking and fondling my left breast. Glorious, absolutely glorious. I felt his manhood pressing into me, and I lost it, I couldn't take it anymore, so I flipped him over and got on top of him; I needed him inside me now, it had been wayyyy too long. As I was riding him slowly, taking him in as deeply as I possibly could, I felt like I couldn't get close enough, I wanted to be truly *inside* this man. I was getting closer, and the slow ride turned into an all-out rollercoaster and finally, much to my neighbors' dismay, I screamed Simon's name and a few other choice words (hoping to god that I wasn't giving the pervert across the way more material). After my performance, Simon took over. I was in heaven; I sank deeper and deeper into the softness of my plush bed as Simon's body melted into mine over and over again...pure, absolute bliss.

I must have passed out, because I woke up with the worst cotton-mouth and a raging headache, not remembering anything after "bliss." Oh no! I had never taken Trouble out; her bladder must have been ready to burst. I jumped out of bed, feeling super-woozy and like a horrible mother. We went for a quick walk and then I got back into bed.

As I looked over at Simon, I felt a bit ill; what the hell was I doing after what he'd done to me? I felt so mixed up and strange—actually, more like sad and disturbed. Why couldn't I just enjoy last night and let it be just that—good time and move on? Well, probably because I was in love with the guy, DUH! I still couldn't shake what he had done to me; I couldn't get it out of my mind. Was this truly what I wanted, to live with him? And if it was, how could I ever trust him again? Did I really want to put the time into "us" knowing that he might never be able to meet my emotional needs? A good indicator of the future was generally how things had gone in the past. Letting him move in meant forgiving him for being unfaithful; I knew he had kissed her and I was sure he'd slept with her. I had to let it all go, which didn't sit well with me…at all! *This is all too much to consider right now, wait until you're thinking clearly and the alcohol is out of your system!*

"Morning, sweetie."

Lovely soft lips were kissing my neck and shoulders. My mind went blank and doubts dissipated as he started tickling my back; my body was tingling from head to toe. Slowly, his hands trailed a bit lower, lightly brushing over my lips and then pulling away, and then back again, lingering a little longer each time before moving away, the brush now a little firmer, teasing me, and then he started his little circle maneuver which never failed…never…

"Omg…omg…ahhhhhhhhhhhhhhhhhhh…yeahhhhhhhhhh…Simon……I…I…love you…AHHHHHHH!"

Damn, he had done it again! One minute I was depressed and confused about him, and the next minute I was putty in his hands (excuse the pun)—all concerns, GONE. Wow, Simon could wrap me around his fucking finger so easily, literally and figuratively!

CHAPTER 18

So it went. Simon moved in with Trouble and I. Things were fantastic for about a month, and then Simon's antics reared their ugly heads all over again…surprise, surprise!

My family and friends weren't too thrilled that I'd let Simon back into my life, and Pops worried I was confusing drama with love. He spoke about the loneliness of loving someone who wasn't capable of returning your love, which made me realize I was repeating my parents' patterns in my own life.

Emma was out of town, but Lou seemed a bit cold when I told her Simon had moved in. I get it; she was just being protective so I tried not to read too much into it. Plus, neither one of us knew how the future would play out. We were both just caught up in our own little worlds, between boyfriends and jobs we weren't able to hang out as much as before.

Finally—and I mean finally—Lou and I connected so she could fill me in on *her* New Year's Eve story. She told me Matthew let it out of the bag that he was totally into her and had been for ages, which was so great. Then last weekend, when we met for breakfast at Le Pain Quotidien, she revealed they were moving in together! I was so happy for her; she deserved a good guy…finally! It was wild, because I'd never seen her in a serious relationship; she was always the party girl, fluttering about, having fun and dating different guys. Now that she was in total "coupledom" mode, I didn't hear from her as often as I used to.

I mean, we checked in and chatted, but we didn't hang out like before, which was kind of sad. I had a really good feeling about this one, and started calling wedding bets early.

After a few weeks of shacking up, though, my personal honeymoon was slowly unraveling. It began with little things, like Simon making plans and *not* including (or even sharing them!) with me. Not really co-habitating couple behavior. It was pretty obvious that my expectations and Simon's were very different—at opposite ends of the spectrum, actually. It was not like we were supposed to be tied at the hip, but it was just disrespectful; after all, we weren't just roommates, we were a committed couple.

Shouldn't it have been common courtesy to talk about plans together? When I shared my feelings about the situation, he didn't understand; he kept repeating that just because we lived together didn't mean we had to hang out all the time or tell each other every move we were going to make. That wasn't what I was trying to say; he was missing the bloody point, as per usual. I tried to explain again…again and again…but he didn't get it, and he thought I was being possessive and trying to control him.

Then one day, out of the blue, Simon came home and informed me that his friend Tyler was coming to visit from New Zealand and sleeping on our couch! WTF, and this was the first I was hearing about it?

On our way to the airport (yes, we had to pick him up as well), Simon revealed he had told Tyler he could stay with us as long as he needed to, until he found a place to live. So now…Tyler was moving in with us? I could feel my blood pressure rising rapidly, I was livid.

His entire pathetic explanation went something like, "So…um… well…Tyler doesn't really have anywhere to stay, so I said he could stay on our couch…um, you don't mind, do you?"

How could he dare spring this on me at the very last second? How I could say no? It was a bit late—of course, he planned it that way, very manipulative. We got into a huge fight as we were pulling into the airport; great, what a way to meet the poor guy. Tyler begged and begged me to let him stay, supposedly Simon owed him a favor; he promised it wouldn't be for very long. I tried to chill out a bit because this was Simon's doing, not Tyler's; he was the innocent bystander in all this.

Tyler stayed with us for three weeks and it actually turned out to be a good thing; he was a really great guy. We would sit for hours chatting, drinking, reading, or just goofing off, and it became pretty apparent I had more in common with Tyler than I did with Simon.

The somber day arrived when Tyler came home and told us he found an amazing guesthouse to move into. He could live there for free, as long as he took care of the pool and did all the gardening—wow, fantastic deal! Needless to say, I was bummed. He had brought such life to our home, and now it seemed so quiet; even Trouble missed him. She had kept whining and pulling clothes out of his bag when he was packing, and we were all cracking up. Funny how things happen—I never wanted him here in the first place and he had become the glue that kept our little apartment happy and semi-functional.

Simon was great at being intimate for a very short time, but he wasn't cut out for the long haul. Every now and then we would have amazing times, but these bouts of happiness were short lived, because it was only a matter of time until Simon pulled another one of his selfish maneuvers.

One lovely Saturday morning, we were hanging out in bed with Simon's head resting on my stomach, while Trouble was napping in his lap. Earlier, while Simon was still asleep, I crawled under the covers to give him a good morning "seeing to", which turned into a long overdue lovemaking session. All was well in our world; we hadn't had a morning like this in ages, and I thought (or *assumed*) a glorious day was in store for us. *I'll make blueberry pancakes with peanut butter, bacon, coffee, and a fresh fruit shake. Then, maybe later we can go for a ride on his bike down the coast and hike in Malibu Canyon. I'm in heaven...*

"Simon, how about blueberry pancakes for breakfast? I'm starving."

"Oh my god, what time is it?"

"What? Why?"

"I've gotta get up, I have to meet Alex at 10:00."

"What?!!"

"Alex and I are going bike riding in Santa Monica."

"What?!"

"Why do you keep saying *what*? Alex and I are taking our bikes to the beach and going bike riding in Santa Monica; why is that so confusing?"

From heaven to hell in mere seconds. Un-fucking-believable.

"I thought we'd hang out, it's Saturday and such a beautiful day..."

"Sylvie, just because we live together doesn't mean we have to spend every waking minute together...."

"We don't! We rarely spend any time together anymore! Why didn't you tell me?"

"What? I'm not allowed to hang out with my friends?"

"I can't believe you're making it about that. I could care less if you hang out with your friends. That's not the issue. When you make plans, it would be nice to let me know so I'd have a clue what's going on, that way I don't wrongly assume that we're hanging out together, since we haven't seen each other all frickin' week."

"I can't believe you're making such a big deal about me hanging out with Alex!"

"I don't care if you hang out with Alex, just communicate with me! I'm your fucking girlfriend, not your roommate!"

He walked out of the bedroom, slamming the door so hard that the walls shook. Trouble jumped up, looking at me with huge, sad eyes. She hated when we argued, which was more often than not these days.

That was the last of our communication, if that's what you wanted to call it, until he was ready to leave. I stayed in bed with Trouble while he was banging around, doing lord knows what. I kept hoping that he'd apologize, tell me that he knew he was being insensitive, and cancel his plans with Alex so we could hang out together; at least let me know he understood where I was coming from. I was fighting back the tears, because I didn't want to cry while he was still there. Trouble knew I was upset and kept licking my face; sweet thing, I loved her.

He finally came back into the bedroom, and got dressed without even looking at me. He sat on the bed to put on his shoes on, and leaned over to kiss me goodbye.

"Bye sweetie, I'll see you later."

Sweetie—like nothing had happened!

He planted a kiss on my tight, annoyed lips. "I don't know when I'll be back; we might go to Casa Vega later, I'll call you."

I pulled away, jumped out of bed and went straight into the bathroom, not saying a word. I heard him put a plate in the sink and then slam the front door.

Trouble hung with me all day, running errands, blah, blah, blah, stuff. Nothing to write home about. I kept checking my phone, thinking he would call, but nothing. Emma was out of town visiting family and Lou was pretty much in her own little world, so I was feeling sad and lonely. When Trouble and I went for our third walk, I ran into the mailman. Aside from bills and more bills, I got a letter from Emma;

she had a thing about writing letters because she thought email was too impersonal. Yikes, it was fifteen pages long—that girl liked to write!

I curled up on the couch with Trouble and my letter. Emma had rushed out of town so fast that she had forgotten to tell me what happened with Jerome, so the first half of the letter was just to fill me in. She had gone out with him the night before she left, and found out that White Shoes *was*, in fact, his girlfriend. She was totally bummed, and told him that she had no desire to see him as long as he was spoken for. She had blown Trevor off shortly after the hair-shaving incident. Their same old crap had popped up again, so they decided it was best to go their separate ways. She was back to being single...or so I thought until I got to page nine of her letter...

There, on page nine, was the outline of a hand—but the middle finger was quite a bit shorter than the others. Oh boy, what happened here? As I continued to read, I started laughing so hard I was crying. Trouble was staring at me with her head cocked sideways, not knowing what the heck was going on.

The finger story went like this: Emma crossed paths with an old flame in London, Leon, and they'd been hanging out quite a bit lately. He worked in a restaurant, and after close one night they were chilling out, having drinks and dancing. They ended up naked on the large oak table in the back of the restaurant, romping like bunnies. All was going splendidly—until the table leg collapsed, sending the table straight to the ground and crushing her fingers. She must have been grabbing the side of the table for maximum thrusting leverage. She said blood was spurting everywhere, and while inspecting the damage she noticed a part of her finger was cut off. They were frantically searching for it, but couldn't find it anywhere; not surprising, since they were totally wasted and most likely in shock. At last, Leon found the little stub and rushed Emma to the hospital.

I couldn't even imagine this scene…both of them, walking into the emergency room, with Emma's hand squirting blood everywhere and Leon carrying the detached bit of her finger. I knew it wasn't funny, but Emma made it hilarious. They were admitted right away, thank goodness. They shot morphine straight into her finger, and she had all the nurses in hysterics with the whole wacky story. The only person I knew that would be giggling in an emergency room with half a finger would be Emma.

Once they got her sufficiently doped up, they informed her that they wouldn't be able to re-attach that small piece of her finger. At that, Emma lost it…she went into actress mode…she cried and pleaded with them to please re-attach the tip of her finger; it was crucial, because she was a concert pianist!

Oh my god, I was dying, I almost peed my pants I was laughing so hard. Where the hell did she come up with that one? That girl was lucky, because it worked, they managed to reattach the little morsel—but it still wasn't normal, hence the shorter finger of her traced hand. Brilliant, what a story! I adored her, she was such an original and very entertaining, to say the least. Why the heck did she wait until the last few pages to tell me this important news; I mean, geez, it should have been the first thing she wrote about!

She mentioned she'd be home in about a month, I couldn't wait. I really missed her, and could definitely use a friend. That letter was a godsend, it put a huge smile on my face; it couldn't have come at a better time. After reading the letter and taking a nap, I decided it was time to have some fun and enjoy the gorgeous day. A distraction was exactly what the doctor ordered, plus, I needed a shoulder to cry on.

(HAPTER 19

As I'd hoped, Dylan was happy to hear from me and wanted to hang out. We hadn't seen each other since our escapade on New Year's Eve, but we'd spoken on the phone a few times. I hadn't thought it was appropriate to see him, since I was trying to work on things with Simon, but suddenly I was feeling different…very different. I tried to shake the feeling that I was using him , but I really enjoyed his company.

He suggested taking a ride on his bike up the coast to watch the sunset. Fantastic idea, exactly what I needed; I loved being on a bike, it cleared away the cobwebs and made me feel so alive and happy.

We took Sunset to PCH and stopped at Gladstone's for a bite; we were both starving and I needed a drink. It was a beautiful warm evening, so we sat outside. It was the usual zoo, but we got lucky—a family was leaving as we walked up, and we snagged their table.

Dylan seemed a little nervous; I could tell he wanted to say something and then the words came out fast and clumsy.

"Sooooo…um…uh……what's the…a…um…the…story with you and Simon?"

"Oh no, it's such a long story, and I really don't want to get into it right now. We're definitely not in a good place."

"That's cool, I understand, you seem a bit distracted and sort of sad. I must admit, the mere fact that you wanted to get together made me think something was up."

"I don't know…yeah, I don't know…it's just…well…it's uhhh… odd…"

"What's odd? Geez, come on, talk to me. I'm your friend, for god's sake!"

"I just don't understand what's going on; I mean I do, it's the same old thing and I'm an idiot. It's, well…I mean…it feels like…it feels like shit! Like it's all falling apart…again, and I'm not happy."

"What do you mean, like shit and falling apart? You? Him? The both of you? The relationship? I can assume what you mean, but c'mon, you *can* tell me."

"Us! It's US! The relationship! That's exactly it! The problem is he has no concept of *us*. It's all about HIM! Occasionally, when he's in the mood, an *us* will exist, but it's generally short-lived, then back to *him* again. It gets old, I feel like I don't know if I'm coming or going. Hot-- --cold---hot---cold."

"What are you talking about, "him"--- "us"----- hot------ cold? Now I'm really confused. What exactly are you trying to say?"

"Geez, it's amazing, are all guys this thick? Isn't it obvious what I'm saying?"

"Hey, don't get funky with me! You aren't being clear and I want to understand. Are you trying to say that you're lonely in the relationship and you don't feel like the two of you are a couple?"

"Yes, yes! That's it. I'm sorry, I didn't mean to go off on you, I'm just soooooo frustrated with him…and myself. You explained exactly how I've been feeling!!!! I'm living with someone who I'm in love with, but feeling totally alone and sad most of the time. Only one party is maintaining the relationship, and it's ME! Am I expecting too much?"

"I don't think there's a right or wrong answer here, it's how you *feel*. If it doesn't feel right, or comfortable for you, that's all that really matters. Perhaps you both want different things; it simply may not be a good fit. This is all exactly what you've told me before, and it sounds like nothing's changed."

"You don't think it's me expecting too much?" For someone who didn't want to talk about it, I was certainly spilling my guts.

"Listen, I'm not in the relationship, so I don't know. I'm just saying if you aren't happy, that's something you need to look at."

Wow, impressive, he was quite perceptive and very wise.

"You guys haven't even lived together that long and you're already feeling this way? I don't want to meddle, but why are you staying if things are so bad?"

"*Hello!* The question of the hour. I'm so pissed off at myself for letting him move in…Uhhh, as far as I'm concerned, it's over!"

"Right, but does *he* know it's over?"

"Well…um…not yet…but I'm sure he has a good idea after this morning."

"Do what you gotta do, but just know that there are great guys out there that will treat you the way you deserve to be treated."

"You think?" I giggled.

"Yep, I'm sure of it," he responded, with a huge grin.

The sunset was amazing; I held my breath and packed in as many wishes as I could before it vanished into the ocean. Pops showed me that little trick when I was little, and I still did it every time I watched the sun go down. Dylan and I hung out for hours, stuffing our faces, people watching, and laughing—what a lovely evening. I was relieved he didn't ask any more Simon questions, because he was the last person I wanted to think about.

When Dylan dropped me off, he hugged me tight and reassured me that everything would work out as it should, and told me to call him if I needed to chat. I really appreciated that he didn't try to kiss me; at this point, I just needed a friend.

I walked into a dark apartment. Obviously Simon had never come home; it was almost eleven-fucking-thirty!

"Come on, Trouble, we're going for a walk, and I need to explain to you why your father will be moving out." I grabbed Trouble's leash, and we marched out the door.

(HAPTER 20

Having a dog is a blessing in so many ways, but the one in disguise was having to walk her all the time. It could be a total pain when I wasn't in the mood, like right then, when I just wanted to get into bed, but it was very therapeutic once I got my ass outside and just did it!

When we got close to home, Trouble pulled her usual stunt, looking dead forward and quickening her pace as she tried to walk right past our apartment. She must have thought I was pretty naïve, like I wasn't going to notice when we walked past our home. It was pretty amusing. Every now and then I went along with it, but tonight wasn't one of those times; I was too pissed off and hurt that Simon wasn't home yet.

I was so wound up that I couldn't get to sleep, so a bath was the next best option. Whenever I took a bath, Trouble tried to hop in with me; she made such a mess that I usually didn't let her, but tonight I didn't care. She jumped in and went crazy, splashing about; the bathroom was a total disaster, water was everywhere. At last, she settled down and plopped right on my stomach. OH…really? I couldn't help laughing, too adorable.

We sat in that position for so long that all the bubbles had disappeared and the water was getting cold. It was time to get out and change venues. After I cleaned up the flood, I put on my comfy, funky flannel pajamas that had been around the block a few times. A rip here, a hole there, missing buttons and a droopy ass, poor things hadn't seen the light of day since Simon had moved in.

"Time for bed, Trouble." She hopped onto the bed and curled up at my feet. She'd lost her space next to me with Simon in the picture, but screw him—I decided it was time for her to reclaim it.

"Come here, Trouble," I patted the spot beside me and instantly her head shot up, ears wiggling, but she didn't move.

"Come on honey, come here, you can sleep next to me…this is where *you* belong."

She got up, took one step, and then stopped, staring at me to make sure I understood what I was saying.

"Yes, this is your place now, come on."

She got it, and couldn't get there fast enough to snuggle up next to me. We spooned together like we used to, before the nuisance moved in. It was now almost 2:00 AM.

"Night, Trouble, I love you."

Oh NO. "Electric legs" were setting in. I tossed and turned and couldn't get comfortable; my legs felt like there were massive electric currents pulsating through them, I couldn't keep them still, and then the itchy-nervous thing started. It felt like I was having a panic attack in my legs. I think it was called restless leg syndrome, I'd seen it on TV, but that was bullshit it was more like electric-fucking legs syndrome—get it right damn it!

I popped out of bed and jogged around the apartment a few times, and then did jumping jacks in the living room. Trouble followed, watching me intensely with her head cocked to one side, wondering what the hell had happened to her mother. I tried everything to exhaust myself, but nothing worked. It was approaching 5:00 AM, so I got back into bed, hoping to finally pass out—but then monkey brain kicked in. *Where the hell was Simon, what is going on?* I couldn't win;

my brain was on fire, my legs were on fire…the worst! Eventually I fell asleep, but kept having intense, horrible dreams about Simon. Around 8:00 AM I decided this sleep wasn't even worth it, so I lugged myself up to talk Trouble for a walk.

Our walk was pretty eventful; Trouble saw a group of children, and practically pulled my arm out of the socket, struggling to get to them. She went crazy from their attention, licking and jumping on them—she absolutely loved kids. She unintentionally knocked a few down, but they just laughed. This incident confirmed I *really* needed to get her into doggie training, because obviously I couldn't seem to control her…around children anyway.

I was zonked after our walk so I tried to get some sleep, but I just tossed and turned all over again. I needed to do something constructive, so I got up and started packing Simon's stuff. I was almost finished when the phone rang—it was a private number. I had a sneaking suspicion it was probably Simon. I really wasn't in the mood to speak to him, but I didn't want to give him the easy way out, leaving a voicemail. I wanted him to have to deal with me directly.

"Hello."

"Uhh, Sylvie, uh…um…it's me, did I wake you?"

"No."

"Errrr…I…I…I'm sorry…I…didn't call…um…last night, I…uhhh…ummm…are you okay?"

"Nope, what's your story?"

My voice was cold as ice.

"I got too wasted with Alex last night, so I stayed over."

"Right, whatever."

"Hey, come on. Don't start, I don't need this right now, I feel like shit."

"YOU don't need this…"

I had to stop myself and calm the hell down, or this call would be all about me being the possessive bitch and *not* about his not calling or coming home last night. He had a unique talent turning things around to avoid taking responsibility for his behavior. This time, I was going to let him bury himself on his own.

"I'm not going to get into this over the phone; I'll talk to you when you get home."

With that, I hung up on him…so much for keeping my cool. Somewhere, in those few seconds, I decided a proper breakup needed to happen in person, not on the phone. I knew damn well that if I did it over the phone, he would disappear for lord knows how long, and I would have to keep his crap until he decided to come get it—which could be ages. I wanted him and his stuff out of my life, TODAY!

Tomorrow needed to be a fresh new day.

(HAPTER 21

Within twenty minutes, Simon had burst through the door.

"What the hell? You hung up on me? I try to call and talk to you, but you just hang up on me. You make such a big thing out of everything. You need to just mellow out!"

"Really, mellow out?"

It was really tough trying to keep it together. I wanted to wring his neck and fire off a few choice words, but no, I stayed put on the couch. Trouble was next to me and didn't budge; usually she would have been all over him, but she must have sensed what was up and wasn't so thrilled with him either.

I started out calmly, but then all hell broke loose.

"This is interesting; you stay out all night, without even calling, and you tell me I overreact about everything? You're so damn manipulative, Simon. Then I'm supposed to feel sorry for *you* because you're hungover? You tell me YOU don't need it? YOU DON'T NEED IT?! Fuck YOU! I'm the one that doesn't need this! I'm sick of this shit. You seem to be under the impression that you're the only one that matters in this relationship. Well, you're dead wrong, buddy!"

I was so full of anger and resentment that I couldn't have stopped myself even if I'd wanted to. He was still by the front door, stunned.

"First you fuck my brains out, and then you jump straight out of bed, informing me that you're going bike riding with Alex and you'd call later," I was on a roll; I didn't even slow down to take a breath, "and that maybe we'd all go to Casa Vega. Trust me, I understand that it was only a *maybe*, so don't use that as an excuse, but you've got fucking fingers—dial the phone and let me know! So *later* comes…and then it goes, with no word from you, NOT A WORD! No call, and THEN you don't even come home last night. Not coming home without calling is unacceptable and totally disrespectful to me and the relationship."

Still no breathing.

"So you FINALLY call, and the moment I start asking questions YOU tell ME to lay off because YOU aren't feeling so hot. FUCK YOU! I'm the one who's owed an explanation and I feel like shit because I haven't slept a wink. So FUCK YOU AGAIN!"

Simon was speechless and his face turned that strange shade of purple I saw on New Year's Eve. He had managed to move from the front door to the overstuffed chair. Trouble was stuck by my side, frozen, probably scared shitless. Simon had a blank look on his face, probably nausea due to his hangover. Too bad; I would've felt sorry for him any other time, but I was totally over it.

"Say something; don't you have ANYTHING to say?"

He sat, looking at his feet, something he seemed to do quite often—usually when he was guilty of something. A thick silence ensued, and then his gaze shifted from his feet to the wall.

"I…I…just don't know…I just…I was having a really great day with Alex and didn't think you'd mind if we didn't meet up last night."

"That is so lame. Like, I wouldn't care that you didn't call and let me know this? Especially considering the funky morning we had. If you would've just called to let me know, that would've been fine, but the problem is that you couldn't even be bothered to check in. AND I'm really burnt on you saying "I don't know" all the time. I've heard you say "I just don't know" so many times that I truly believe you, I realize that you really don't know. You haven't a clue. You don't know yourself or what you want and never have. You've got commitment issues. You can't commit in your heart, so you keep sabotaging the relationship in little ways. Staying out all night without calling is HUGE! I'm sorry, but I don't want this anymore. I don't want to live like this; I'm tired of being unhappy and wishing for more. I know now that I shouldn't have given you another chance after you screwed me over on New Year's Eve, but hindsight is 20/20 and there's nothing I can do about that now."

"I guess I'm just not good at this…this relationship stuff."

"That's all you have to say? Really, Simon? I've had it, that's such bullshit! I used to think you were such a sweet, sensitive, guy, but it's totally selective. You turn on the charm when you want something, but otherwise, forget it, it's all about you."

I had really wanted this to work and I did love him, but I knew in my heart nothing would change. "You've got to get your stuff out of here today."

He had tears rolling down his face. Trouble had picked up on the fact that he was upset and couldn't stay mad at him any longer, so she ran over to him and started licking his face. Poor thing must have been so confused, between the both of us crying and fighting all the time.

I sat expressionless; I gotta tell you, fighting back the tears was no easy task. He was looking at me with those damn puppy dog eyes. It was tough not falling for it, as I always had, but I knew this would keep happening over and over again, and I didn't want to be a constant victim.

Nothing was more nauseating than people who constantly complained about their life, but did nothing about it. The only topic they seemed to enjoy was how miserable they were. It was way too draining, and I had no desire to join that club; I must admit, I'd been dabbling and had come way too close to becoming a new member. That had to end right here.

Even with Simon sitting right in front of me, for some reason I could only think of my former friend Rebecca. Every time Rebecca and I had gotten together, she would rattle on about her horrible boyfriend. She would tell me stories about finding other girls' hair and an occasional earring in her boyfriend's bed—how horrific was that? They'd have plans, but he wouldn't show up, so she'd actually go searching for him and track him down at The Cat and Fiddle or Barney's Beanery. He'd be drunk already, hanging out with his buddies. According to rumor, he had fucked a couple of the waitress in the parking lot one night, yep! The doozy was one evening, at some bar, he took a girl to his car, and, as he went down her, he realized she was a HE! Brilliant! Served him right, but what I really wanted to know was if he actually sucked him off in the end.

When she asked my opinion about what she should do, over and over again, my response was always the same—dump him. Guess what she would say? "But I love him, and I can't be alone."

Nauseating. I completely lost respect. After months of this, I knew I couldn't hang out with her anymore; it was way too draining. I'd spent so many hours on the phone with her, listening, consoling her, trying to help her in any way I could, and there were hundreds of Don Cuco and El Coyote therapy dinners as well. It was just way too depressing, and I wanted nothing to do with her until years later, when she finally ended it with him. I knew it was time for me to do the same, before this slid off into dangerous Rebecca territory.

"Simon, did you hear what I said?"

"Yes…I know…I'm just not good at this…this isn't for me. Every relationship I've been in hasn't worked. I agree with you, I'll move out."

Wow, that wasn't what I had expected to hear. I mean, he could have at least tried to change my mind or something—not that I would have budged! But still, what an ego shock. He got up and wrapped his arms around me; I felt his tears on my cheek.

"Sylvie, sweetie, I love you so much," his voice cracked, and tears were running down his face. "I…I…I've never been happier with anyone: waking up next to you, eating breakfast, reading in bed, cuddling, all of it, I love being with you…but I feel trapped. When we get too close, I feel like I'm losing myself, and I freak out. I'm scared to go too deep, so I pull away—so yes, I think you're right, we should end this. If we don't, you'll end up hating me, and your love and friendship is way too important to me."

This was way too gut-wrenching and bittersweet. We were hanging on to each onto each other, with tears streaming down our faces; we couldn't bear to look at each other, it was way too intense.

He was the first to speak.

"Is it okay if I move my things out tomorrow? Would it be alright if I stayed tonight, one last night, so we can talk and cuddle?"

I couldn't even believe I said it, but the words blurted out.

"Yes, you can stay tonight."

We were wiped out, so we watched TV, had some leftovers, and went to bed early. When we got into bed we talked about stuff, reminiscing about the good times and how sad it was that we were separating. We knew it was for the best and at least we had given it a damn good try. I wasn't sure if this was therapeutic or making it worse, but at least it was a proper closure.

Right before I fell asleep, I had an epiphany. I wasn't exactly exempt from being a commitment-phobe, myself. Tonight had been the first time I'd actually opened up to him and was completely transparent. I guess I had felt safe, now that it was actually over. At the end of the day, it seemed we had more in common than we thought we did. I guess you could call us Mr. & Mrs. Parker Brothers; serious game-players. He wasn't the only guilty one here, he was just more obvious about it than I was.

Morning came too quickly. I had halfway expected him to say he changed his mind about things; beg me for forgiveness, tell me that it was all a mistake, that we should try to work things out. He didn't, so my ego was suffering considerably. Mixed emotions on this one; I wanted him to want me but I didn't want him anymore. Games, again...

"Good morning, that was a lovely cuddle. Do you want some coffee?"

He seemed so cheerful. I just glared at him. How could he be so spunky? We had just broken up, for heaven's sake!

"How can you be so happy after last night? You never cease to amaze me."

"I'm just trying to keep it together. Come on, don't get weird, you were so chill last night."

"Unbelievable," I muttered under my breath, and went into the bathroom.

I was hurt. I couldn't help it; how could he act like nothing happened? I started crying, but now I *really* knew I had made the right decision. I sat on the toilet for what seemed like ages, completely dazed and heartbroken. What a dick; he didn't even check on me to see if I was okay.

Finally, he knocked, but *only* to tell me that he was leaving. I didn't open the door, and he didn't ask me to. Why was I *still* surprised by his behavior? I was endlessly expecting him to act differently.

"I'm leaving; I'll be back later to get my stuff. What are you doing in there?"

I didn't say a word. He waited about ten seconds for a response and then he left; I heard the front door open and close. Not even a slam; he wasn't even slightly agitated or hurt! AHHHHhhhhh. Now the fierce, shoulder-shaking, heart-wrenching, loud bawling started and wouldn't stop; I just wailed. I was already so sick of crying.

Moping around the apartment, trying to get a grasp on myself, I decided I didn't want to be home when he returned. I took Trouble for a walk and then we drove to the supermarket; I needed junk food for this crisis. I cruised up and down every aisle, grabbing Captain Crunch, Peanut M&Ms, Rocky Road ice cream, chocolate chip cookies, Snickers…and then carrots, apples, and salad-in-a-bag, to alleviate the guilt.

When I finished junk food shopping, I drove slowly by the carport to see if Simon's bike was there; damn, there it was. I decided to go to the park. Trouble and I frolicked for a bit, but I was wiped out and wanted to go home and relax. As we pulled up, I was praying he was gone—but no such luck.

"Hey, what's up?"

Trouble and I walked in with the groceries, and I tried to act like I didn't have a care in the world.

"What are you doing?"

"I'm packing up my stuff. Bert's coming over in a bit with his van."

"Are you sure this is what you want?" The words shot out of my mouth before I could lasso them back in. Where the hell did that come from? I had no self-control.

"Sylvie, come on, we decided…"

"I know, but are you sure?" Why was I trying to get him to change his mind or doubt his decision? My ego obviously couldn't handle that he wanted to leave ME as much as *I* wanted him to leave.

He sighed as he sat down. "No, I'm not positive, but I feel like we have to do this. I'm pretty sure I'll probably regret it, but this doesn't seem to be working for either of us."

"I know, you're right." I grabbed my keys, and on the way out I gave him a warm hug. "I want you to know that I love you and I'm really sad it didn't work."

So cliché. With that, I walked out the door. Trouble could keep him company while he packed. I had no desire to watch him move. That would be way too painful. Going to the gym was a much better option. There, done; I had put Mrs. Parker Brothers to bed and gotten closure on our relationship, once and for all.

CHAPTER 22

When I returned a few hours later, he was gone and so was most of his stuff; a few things remained, his stereo and a few knick-knacks. What really killed me was the huge gap in my closet—which under different circumstances, I would have been totally thrilled about, because now my dresses were able to breathe again. It summed up exactly the void I was feeling, so I immediately spread out my clothes, attempting to get my life back to normal as soon as possible.

Suddenly, I remembered Simon and I had plans to go to a beach party in Orange County. Although I wasn't exactly in a party mood, I knew it was a good idea to force myself to go.

It was the perfect day for a beach party; the sun was always good therapy. I wasn't feeling very social, so after doing the rounds I pretty much kept to myself, soaking up the rays and enjoying some beers.

"You don't look so good."

"Geez, thanks. Now I feel even better."

"I didn't mean it that way…you just aren't your usual spunky self. What are you doing over here by yourself?"

Jake was standing above me, smoking a cigarette. He was a friend of a friend, who I had heard through the grapevine had a bit of a thing for me, but I couldn't ever be bothered. I was under the impression he was a womanizer, and that was something I *never* wanted to deal with.

"Just a bit down. Simon and I broke up yesterday."

Jake and Simon had met at a mutual friend's wedding a few

months back. Jake had made it very obvious to Simon that he had a crush on me, which I thought was fantastic, because Simon was in one of his detached modes. Later, in our hotel room, Simon kept going on and on about the gall of Jake flirting with me in front of him. He thought Jake was a jerk. Of course he did.

"I'm sorry; he seemed like a nice guy."

"Yeah, well, he moved out today. I'm not in the best headspace."

"I've got an idea. I just bought a boat; we could go out on it tomorrow. It might cheer you up."

"Thanks, but I don't think so. I wouldn't be such great company, but I appreciate you asking."

"Okay, I understand, but why don't you give me your number, and I'll call you in the morning to see how you feel. If you're not up to it and don't want to go, then I won't pressure you, but who knows, you may want to."

"Okay, that works," I had always found him terribly attractive, but the whole womanizer vibe put me off. "I'm off, I'm wiped out."

"Okay, but I'm definitely calling you tomorrow morning. I really think you'll have a blast on my boat, and I would love for you to come."

He walked me to my car, asked me for my keys, and proceeded to unlock and open my car door for me—very good impression! He made sure I was all strapped in before he leaned in and kissed me on the cheek.

"Don't take this the wrong way, but I'm excited you're available again. Have a safe drive, speak to you tomorrow."

Oh my! My heart was racing a hundred miles an hour the entire way home. He got to me, damn it; I was enticed. This was so exciting—what were the chances that the day after I broke up with my boyfriend, someone would ask me out to take the edge off my grief? I wasn't going to let the womanizer thing concern me right now, I just wanted and needed to have some fun, and the ego boost was bonus. This whole Simon situation had annihilated my confidence, and it was time to repair it.

I walked in the door feeling pretty good about myself, and then my heart sank. The rest of his stuff was totally cleared out; he apparently had come back and got *all* of it. I thought he had left a few things so he would have an excuse to come back, but obviously not. This hit me like a ton of bricks; so much for my short-lived grief reprieve.

(HAPTER 23

I didn't get an ounce of sleep that night. I tossed and turned with disturbing dreams all night, and by morning, I didn't feel so hot. I was making my way out the door with Trouble when my phone rang. I couldn't be bothered to answer; that was what voicemail was for.

"Hey Sylvie, it's Jake, I'm checking in to see how you're feeling. It's about 8:00, and I'll be around for a while, so give me a call."

Eh. I'd call him and let him know I wasn't up to it after I got back from our walk.

The phone was ringing as we walked in.

"Hey, what's up? You feel better today?"

Boy, was he persistent.

"Hi, I'm okay. In a funk, but okay–"

He cut me off, "Then I *really* think you need to come out today. I have some food and–"

I interrupted, "I don't think so; I wouldn't be such great company, but I appreciate the invitation. I would love to come on another day..."

Now he cut me off—geez, we were interrupting each other right and left!

"Listen, come on, you need some cheering up, plus it's a beautiful day..."

"But..."

He cut me off AGAIN; this was beginning to piss me off, and I realized he wasn't going to take no for an answer.

"…and I already bought all sorts of food for a picnic. I have cheese, crackers, fruit, sandwiches, beer, wine, and whatever else you want me to get."

I gotta say, it was beginning to sound pretty good. I couldn't believe he'd already packed a picnic—that was very sweet. I mean, why sit and wallow in this empty apartment anyway?

"What time are you going?"

"Does that mean you're coming?"

"Yep, why not, it sounds fun."

"Just come when you're ready…how long do you think that will be? Roughly? I've already got the boat at the house ready to go, hoping that you'd say yes."

"It'll take me about forty-five minutes to get ready and forty-five to get there."

"Great, so I'll see you between 10:30 and 11:00. Cheer up, we'll have a blast. See ya then."

Crisis—what the heck should I wear? I frantically rifled through my clothes, and came up with something perfect for the occasion: a playful short skirt and skimpy tank top. It was cutesy-sexy, without being obvious.

After I got ready, I was starting to get excited. I blasted the stereo and flew down the freeway to his house; I couldn't get there fast enough.

I made it in good time, but when I pulled up, the butterflies in my stomach were going nuts. He looked so damn sexy in his trunks, I about lost it, and then I saw his boat—it was a cigarette boat! Speedboats made me weak in the knees; throw in a few beers and I was a happy girl.

He was a bloody maniac. We were speeding like crazy through the waves, and I truly thought we were going to flip; going these speeds in the ocean was totally different than on the lake. Every time we hit a wave I thought the boat was going to bust in half or flip backwards. I felt so alive and exhilarated, and just scared enough to get my adrenaline pumping.

We went to the bay and ate lunch on the beach. He had gone all out: ham, turkey, roast beef, three kinds of cheese, fruit, cookies, chips, crackers, and, of course, wine and beer. Wow, he had thought of everything. Beautiful beach, great food, being taken care of by a handsome man? I felt like I was floating on a cloud. I was experiencing a super-intense, crystal clear euphoria that was so unbelievably amazing, I felt like I was flying.

I'd had a couple glasses of wine, so I felt a little giddy and was ready for more intense wave action. This time he let me drive; I was pretty sure I scared the shit out of him. I went absolutely insane, flying through the waves and pulling radical U turns. It was such a rush!

When he kissed me goodbye, I melted; what a wonderful end to a fantastic day.

"Drive safe and text me when you get home. I had a great time today, you're one amazing woman; Simon totally blew it letting you go!"

"Thank *you* for a fantastic day. I feel so much better, and I have you to thank for it. I really appreciate it."

He leaned in and kissed me again. As I pulled away, I noticed him still standing in the street, watching me as I drove off. Damn, I was falling, I was hooked; I wanted more where *that* came from. What an extraordinary day.

(HAPTER 24

Jake and I couldn't get enough of each other. His presence certainly helped take the edge off the Simon grieving process. I felt like a queen; he wined and dined me, never letting me pay for a thing—unlike Simon, who had always wanted to split everything.

We went out on the boat most weekends, spending as much time together as possible. It was a little bit of a challenge, since I lived in LA and he lived in Huntington, but we managed pretty well.

He was always surprising me with little gifts, and the gifts started getting larger. One day he asked to borrow my car, and when we met up later he surprised me with a new sound-system and speakers! I couldn't believe it, what had I done to deserve all this? I had gone from Simon famine…to Jake feast! Unbelievable, no guy had ever done things like this for me before. I was one fortunate girl—I could get used to this.

That speedboat was a total aphrodisiac for me; I was completely obsessed with being on the ocean as much as possible. Flying through the waves always made me horny, and having sex on the boat was insane; there was nothing like being naked in the sun. Then we'd go back to his house and go at it again. I was having a total blast, but that little voice in my head kept saying *no future*.

There was something I just didn't trust about him, and to be honest, our relationship was pretty shallow. It was all about fun: sex, drinking, gifts, expensive dinners, blah, blah, blah. There wasn't a lot of substance there. Our connection was so hot that there was no way it could sustain itself; it had to burn out eventually. He told me he loved me after a week! I mean, I got that I was totally lovable and all, but way too soon. He even had Josh the Jerk beat on that one.

Jake stories started to surface early on, but I pushed the playboy ones right out of my head–he was so into me, he couldn't possibly have time for anyone else. Eventually, I did hear some news that hit home. Supposedly, he was very intense (duh), obsessive (yea…), infatuated (absolutely), and passionate (mmhmm) in the beginning of relationships…but cooled down after a few months.

Paranoia was setting in. I started wondering when the ball would drop, realizing it was only a matter of time until he grew bored with me and moved on to a new challenge. I was a bit frightened; I couldn't handle another blow so close to the last one. Once I realized what I was up against, I tried to back off and not *feel* so much. As anyone knows, this is virtually impossible unless you are a robot. All it did was create exactly what I didn't want to happen; it was a self-fulfilling prophecy.

They say when rebound relationships don't work out, you feel the pain of the first breakup AND the pain of the second, all at once. In other words, deal with your shit and get over the first relationship before you get into another one. Good advice too late; I was an anxious mess. Simon kept calling, but I was so into Jake that I blew him off.

The cooling-off kicked in around the two-and-a-half-month mark. Jake started spending more time with friends on the weekends and not coming to LA as often, using the excuse that he was tired. Very odd, why wasn't he tired before? There also seemed to be a lack of interest in our speedboat escapades, which was actually quite depressing. It was without-a-doubt happening, and it felt worse than I could have imagined.

Although I knew intellectually this had nothing to do with me, I started questioning everything and endlessly beating myself up. I wondered if I had done something to cause his loss of interest, blah, blah, blah. What I was able to acknowledge were the positive aspects of our short relationship; it *had*, in fact, helped me get over the initial pain of the Simon breakup, and I'd had a blast!

The last night that Jake and I went to dinner, I was totally not into it. It had been a long day, and I was losing interest in this liaison as quickly as he was.

Dinner dragged on because we really didn't have much to say to each other, and I was drinking a lot of wine to get through it. He was drinking a lot faster than usual, and started getting belligerent and pissy with the waiter. That was a side of him I'd never seen, and it was extremely embarrassing.

After a series of awkward silences, he got up and walked over to a woman at the bar, proceeding to talk to her for ten minutes and leaving me alone at the table. What sent me over the edge was when they exchanged phone numbers—how fucking rude!

Okay, that was the last straw. Things had been going downhill for a while, so that seemed like a good breaking point. There wasn't even anything left to hang out for; the excitement was definitely gone, and he didn't seem to give a shit about me anymore anyways.

Watching him walk back to the table, I decided it was time to get my life in order. I needed to be alone—no Simon, and certainly NO JAKE. I had to stop running from my pain and face it head on, by myself!

I got up and told him that I was ready to go. It wasn't even worth talking about. I didn't care about fixing it, or even getting a reaction out of him. I was done.

"What! What the fuck? Can't I fucking talk to another chick? We aren't fucking married; I can talk to anyone I want! Don't be such a fucking bitch. We never talked about not dating other people. We can do what we want..."

He kept rambling on. He was drunk and disgusting! I instantly went from disliking him to detesting him. I couldn't wait to get out of there.

"Jake, I really don't care who you talk to, I think you're an ass and I don't want anything to do with you anymore. As far as I'm concerned, you can stay here; have fun at the bar and take a taxi home, I'm outta here."

"No, fuck you, I bought this dinner, you can't just bail..."

"Watch me."

He was following me as I walked out of the restaurant, and all of a sudden he violently grabbed my arm and spun me around. Everyone in the restaurant was watching.

"You bitch, you can't just fucking leave like this. Come on, let's talk about it."

"Jake, let go of me, there isn't anything to talk about. It's pretty obvious this relationship has gone way past its expiration date. We're so over, just let go of me."

I jerked away and continued walking to the valet, and he snatched my arm again. I gave the valet my ticket and coldly asked Jake to let go of me. The valet was looking a little concerned; Jake was a big guy, and a large, pissed-off drunk was not someone anyone wanted to reckon with.

Dickhead finally let go of my arm, called me a fucking cunt, and walked off into the sunset. Another beautiful ending, ladies and gentlemen.

"Are you okay, would you like some help here?"

"Thanks, I'm fine. I just need my car, quickly, so I can get out of here before he comes back. I appreciate your concern though."

What a horrible evening. I cried all the way home. I didn't want to feel anything for such an asshole, but I couldn't help it. It was such a shock that he could be such a jerk—how did he hide it for so long?

The exhilaration of being treated like I was the most desirable, gorgeous woman in the world came crashing down. I now felt the complete opposite; my morale was shot to hell.

Time to move on and grow up. I left myself a reminder to call the Women's Clinic on Monday for a much needed and long overdue therapy appointment…

CHAPTER 25

It was a new year all over again. Crazy how time flew when I was being crazy, and as I looked back on the last year, I knew I didn't want a repeat. It was way too tumultuous, relationship-wise anyway. Career-wise, all was pretty constant; thankfully, something was stable. My job was so easy I could do it with my eyes closed. I was starting to think maybe I should be looking for challenges in *this* part of my life, instead of wacked-out men and dramatic relationships. New year, new job…something a little more challenging than temp work. Also on my list of resolutions was to finish the script I had started ages ago—no more lollygagging, I needed to get it done!

All hell broke loose last New Year's Eve, and hadn't let up until almost a year later. I broke up with Simon, made up with Simon, Simon moved in, and then Simon moved out, finally putting an end to a way overdue cycle of madness. I immediately jumped into a whirlwind romance with a complete psycho that crash-landed a few months later, leaving me exhausted and distraught. Thankfully, there had been a few non-eventful months, so I was feeling relaxed and regrouped to start off this new year.

Jake called after that horrendous evening. He apologized, and wanted to pick up where we left off. I told him I wasn't interested, and thanked him for everything—after all, it was fun, and what was the point of holding a grudge? I found out later from a friend of a friend that he was a total alcoholic, and our restaurant incident seemed to be something he did quite often. I was still blown away how he kept it hidden for so long AND why no one warned me about that. Oh well, it didn't matter; I had an awesome time while it lasted. No regrets.

New Year's Eve came and went virtually unnoticed. Trouble and I stayed home, watching movies and eating popcorn. Someone told me that the way you start a new year sets the tone for how the rest of the year will go. Perfect, this was about as calm as New Year's Eve could get.

We rarely got rain in southern California, so when we did it was a nice change and a great excuse to stay home and hibernate; it had been raining for nine days straight, though, and it was getting a bit ridiculous. Thankfully, I was off work, so I didn't have to leave the house and join the crazies on the road. Taking Trouble out for walks wasn't so fun in a monsoon.

We'd just entered rainy day #10, and the water was wreaking havoc everywhere, especially in the canyons; they'd turned into mad, rushing rivers, and homes were sliding down hillsides. It was really sad—I wasn't sure what the heck was going on, but someone in LA must have really pissed someone off in the universe.

With all this crazy weather, I didn't feel guilty about staying in to catch up on my reading. The most recent book I had finished was about setting goals, getting inspired, and staying motivated, which was very apropos. After completing that book, I couldn't wait to sit down and finish my darn script.

I started writing like a mad woman; inspiration was flowing from every pore. I felt like I was totally in the zone. As I came to page seventy-nine, I pressed "Save", and I got a black bomb on my computer screen—a System Error Explosion! Finally, the damn thing reset and I couldn't find page seventy-nine...it only went as high as page three. *No, no, no, no, please no, this can't be happening, don't tell me I lost all those pages!* NO FUCKING WAY!

Panic was setting in, my cheeks were burning and I could feel sweat breaking out all over my body.

"Where did my pages go?" I yelled.

"WHERE DID MY FUCKING PAGES GO, DAMN IT! WHERE ARE MY PAGES?"

Trouble glanced over to see who the heck I was yelling at. I tried to calm down and think clearly. *Yeah right, not happening…*

"Please tell me this isn't true! Please, all this work, it can't be gone. I can't believe this! I read the damn motivational book, I got motivated and wrote all day, and now I lost it all? No, please no!"

"Why, WHY, WHY?"

I kept repeating it over and over again, with my head in my hands.

"Damn computers! Pieces of shit!"

I kept trying to calm myself down, but it wasn't working. The best thing to do was to get away from the computer, walk around, go to the gym. Anything active to get my mind off what just happened, then come back to it with a clear head. I was too worked up to accomplish anything at this point.

Flustered as all hell, I ventured out into the downpour of all down-pours to go to the gym. I was not excited about driving my antique vehicle in such a crazy storm. The wipers weren't that great, and the defroster never seemed to defrost. So I got into my car very pissed off and soaked, when she decided not to cooperate with the program.

R-RRRRRR-HMMMMmm-puuut-puuuut…

I turned the key again and again, but nothing happened. I wanted to scream…so I did, I deserved a good howl, damn it! I let loose; I sat in the car and just screamed my heart out, as loud as I could.

I screamed until I couldn't scream anymore, and I felt a hell of a lot better. In fact, I wanted to do it one more time, just for good measure.

"AHHHHHHHHHHHHHHHHHHHHHHH-
HERRRRRRRRRREEEERRRRRRRRRRRREEEEAHHHHH."

Whew, that felt really good. Lord knows what my neighbors thought, but who cared. I sat back and thought about everything that had transpired so far today. This was definitely NOT my day. My planets, numerology, biorhythms, whatever, they were all messed up, and I just had to deal with it. I sat back, contemplating life, trying to get back on a more positive note.

It was a new year, and I'd been feeling positive about things to come. I had made my new year's resolutions, something I'd *never* done before, and I even wrote them down:

1) *Work on my script, get it finished*
2) *Work out more and eat better, lose bum*
3) *Get a new job to make more money so I can buy a house*

No mention of men, because it was all about me right now; getting my act together would mean attracting a better caliber male. I limited it to three goals so it was realistic and do-able, but, for some reason, today wasn't cooperating. Maybe this was a test, a roadblock to see how serious I *really* was about my new aspirations.

The work I'd done on my script was all in vain—vanished, totally disappeared, nowhere to be found. I tried to go to the gym to work off my big ass but my car wouldn't start, and I couldn't go to the grocery store to buy healthy food because I had no way to get there. It didn't look good, but I had to go with it and remain positive. I needed a hot bath and a glass of wine to calm me down, so I got out of my broken-down jalopy and went back into the house. Trouble devoured me, nothing new there.

As I was sitting in the bath, wine in hand, a philosophical thought came to me about the missing pages; they had vanished because they were supposed to. I was such a different person from when I started that script. I was having a hard time trying to stay on course with what I had written previously; it just wasn't flowing and now I knew why. I needed to start fresh and write the way I felt now, from the person I was today.

Whew, thank you for that revelation, because, after today's events, I'd lost all motivation and was desperately trying to find the proverbial light at the end of the tunnel. Everything happened for a reason, but the tricky part could be locating the darn reason! Many of us couldn't get past the obvious issues, and wallowed in a pissed-off victim mode, as I was doing earlier, the "why does this always happen to me" mind-set, which then attracted even more negative stuff.

Cabin fever was hitting an all-time high. Poor Trouble hadn't had a decent walk in days, but at least I was getting a lot of writing done; in fact, I was back up to page seventy-nine! Whoo-hooo! I was on a roll. AAA came to check out my car, and it was just my battery—easy fix, I bought one from them. Now I was back on track.

When the phone rang, I knew it was Simon. I had no desire to get together with him, not now anyways. He left a message, wanting to hang out; the guy wouldn't quit, he wanted what he couldn't have. Granted, it would be great to see him and get out of the house, but way too dangerous. He has a scary way of pulling me right back in, and, if I were to be brutally honest, I still felt something for him—way too risky. I was in a really good place and had no desire to taint my new happy life, lonely or not.

(HAPTER 26

I couldn't remember the last time I went on a date, and I didn't care; life was good. One day in therapy, it dawned on me that since moving to LA I had gone from one guy to the next, and then to the next, and changed apartments practically every year. How exhausting!

Being alone had been very cathartic and eye-opening. As much as I didn't want to work in the entertainment industry, I got an offer I couldn't refuse. One of the production companies I'd been temping for offered me a full time gig with a great salary and benefits. That inspired me even more to finish my script, because now I had a captive audience to read it. All was falling into place nicely, AND after cutting down on my onion dip and M&M addiction, my ass shrank two sizes. I'm telling you, this no-boyfriend stuff was way better than I thought it would be.

So here I was, single and loving it, when out of nowhere Dylan called me. I never called or saw him again after our Gladstone's adventure, so I was curious what was up—I mean, if I were him, I would have been pretty pissed off with me. Even though I hadn't meant to, I realized I had been pretty selfish and unconcerned with Dylan's feelings.

"Hey, how are you?" I was actually a little nervous.

"Great, it's been ages, what have you been up to? I noticed you were MIA on New Year's Eve."

I started cracking up. "Yeah, after last year's nonsense I decided to lay low."

"Yeah, no kidding. Remember, I was an innocent bystander practically hit by your shrapnel," he said, laughing. "So, what are you doing on this beautiful day?"

"Not much, just catching up on stuff." Boy, did I sound boring. "What about you?"

"Going to the driving range, it's usually not too crowded around now. Do you want to come along? Well…on second thought, maybe not; it might be boring for you."

"No! No, I think it would be fun."

"Excellent, are you ready now?

"Yeah, why not?"

"I'll come by to get you, see you in a few."

How fun, this was a nice change; my idea of having a good time was frequenting El Coyote, Casa Vega, Don Cuco and a few other restaurants and pubs around town…I mean, really? I needed to branch out a bit, there had to be a lot more to life than work, beer, margaritas and Mexican food. Somehow, I had missed that part on my New Year's resolutions list.

I was really excited as we pulled up to the Studio City driving range for two reasons: (1) it was great to see Dylan, and (2) I'd never been to a driving range.

He got a large bucket of golf balls and grabbed a spot at the far end of the range. I sat behind him on the bench, watching all the action; it was fascinating observing everyone as they were hitting balls. Overall, it seemed most people weren't so thrilled with their results; I heard a lot of hemming, hawing, cussing or merely just huge, heaving sighs. I understood that the goal was to hit the ball straight and long, but, more often than not, that wasn't what was happening. They went either too far to the left, too far to the right—or they missed the ball completely, although that was quite rare. Why did these people put themselves through this irritation? It doesn't seem like they were enjoying themselves much.

One guy was so pissed off that he took his club and whacked it so hard on the ground, yelling, "FUCK!" that it actually broke in half. The whole place was staring at him, but he didn't seem to care. He picked up both pieces, placed them in his bag, and pulled out another club, continuing to hit balls like nothing ever happened. I wondered how many clubs he went through in a week.

Dylan, on the other hand, looked like he was doing pretty well; not a lot of complaints coming from his area. I sat back and cheered when they looked good. He grinned and seemed to like it, but everyone else was turning around and giving me dirty looks. I guess I was ruining their concentration. Screw 'em if they couldn't take a joke, they sucked anyway.

What I found really amusing were the women on the range. I'd noticed lately that every woman's magazine was promoting golf as a way to meet men, and the women in Studio City were clearly paying attention. I'm sure all females who golfed weren't trying to pick up a man, but I did spot the three there that were. They were dressed more like they were going out clubbing instead of golfing, wearing super-tight short skirts with extremely revealing tops. The dead giveaway was that they were looking around more than they were hitting balls, and, true to form, men were tripping over themselves to give them golfing tips. The magazines were obviously correct.

"Okay, your turn."

I came back from a heavy space-out just as Dylan was handing me a golf club.

"What? No, I've never golfed before. I don't want to break the club, or whack a ball at someone."

"Don't worry about it, I'll help you."

"Oh boy."

He told me how to stand and how to hold the club, which felt totally unnatural. I felt all contorted and lame.

"Okay, now relax and swing. Feel the club, one smooth motion like a pendulum."

Yeah right, he made it sound so simple; getting my hands and arms in this position was one thing, but then trying to move in this state seemed impossible! I felt like a total idiot, and I was sure I looked like one as well. I tried the movement s-l-o-w-l-y, and attempted a swing—just a practice swing, no ball yet. I felt so stiff and peculiar; how could this be correct?

"Good, good, loosen up and bend your knees slightly, elbows relaxed. Now practice a few more times without hitting a ball."

I tried it several more times, but it still felt weird. I didn't feel like a pendulum, I felt rough and gawky. At that moment, I developed a newfound respect for golfers. I now understood how truly difficult a sport it was. I was even amazed by the golf babes—how could they pull all this off and still look hot?!

"Okay, let me try with a ball this time."

Dylan positioned a ball for me. I tried to relax. I checked my feet, knees, arms, elbows…my heavens, there was a lot to remember; I took a deep breath, and SWUNG!

OMG, I missed the damn ball completely. What a doofus. I looked around and felt like a total twat. I tried to laugh it off, asking Dylan what the heck happened, but I could feel my face turning eggplant purple. I really hated not being able to do something.

"You can do it…lighten up, bend your knees, and take a deep breath…don't be embarrassed, it's your first time. Keep your eye on the ball."

"AhhhhhhHHH! Damn, errrrrrr."

I missed again. This wasn't amusing at all.

"It's okay, Sylvie. It's tough to judge in the beginning. You need to relax; otherwise you'll never be able to hit it."

I was petrified of breaking his golf club, slamming it dead into the ground while I was attempting to hit the ball. I think that was why I kept missing it. Boy, wouldn't he be thrilled if I broke his club. *"Yea, man, I take this chick to the driving range and she busts my club!"* I could see it now. I don't think I was relaxing much.

I was reciting instructions to myself under my breath, wanting so badly to get it right and then WHAM…I did it! I had hit the ball and it flew pretty far *and* straight. I thought Dylan was impressed. Wow, I was!

"See, didn't that feel great? That was a good shot for your first time."

I hit a few more balls, but none came close to *the one*. It was fun, and I could definitely see why people got addicted and obsessed with the game. Dylan confirmed what I figured; it was the random brilliant shots that kept golfers coming back for more. I got it now.

After our driving range experience, we went to Jerry's Deli for beer and nutrition. Dylan asked what was up with Simon, Jake, and whoever else I might have been dating. I filled him in on the various sagas, and he didn't have much to say about any of it. I thought he was glad they were in the past and not in the present for a change. Interesting how he knew about Jake; I guessed he'd been keeping tabs on me.

I could tell Dylan was still into me, but after spending most of the day together, I realized I wasn't into him as much as I thought I was. He felt more like a friend than a crush this time around. When we hung out on New Year's Eve and the day we went out on his bike, I was crushing hard. That "oomph" wasn't there anymore; how could that happen? Perhaps it was because I was enjoying my alone time, and for once I wasn't looking for a quick fix.

It dawned on me that every time I'd been with him in the past, I was upset and in the middle of some kind of drama with Simon. Now that I was feeling pretty good, with no impending crises, he wasn't as appealing to me. Maybe I just didn't want him now that I could have him.

Maybe this was a good sign, and this mellow, pleasant friendship was the key to a healthy relationship. I was willing to keep an open mind and give it a go. What the heck; I had nothing to lose, only to gain…so I thought.

CHAPTER 27

After that day, we were inseparable; we were fast becoming best friends, partners in crime. It was nice, because no one was making any moves, which was exactly what I needed. I needed a break from relationships, no more band-aiding one boyfriend for another. This way I could really get to know Dylan without the usual dating pressures, to see if those passionate feelings for him would return.

Simon continued to call, but I had no desire to see him. The mere fact that I wasn't interested was fueling his fire like crazy, so he wasn't giving up. Once he conquered a woman, that was an entirely different story, but you've heard way too much about that already. It was extremely liberating to know that he had absolutely no effect on me anymore. Thank god. It was about time!

Dylan and I were having dinner at El Compadre one night, and getting quite loopy. Out of nowhere, I burst out, "Let's go to a strip bar! I've never been before, and I'm curious to see what they're like."

"What? Are you serious? Let me guess, more research?"

He was right; I'd been doing intense research on bosoms, because I was considering getting mine enhanced. We must have purchased every "T & A" magazine in circulation; it was crucial to pinpoint precisely what shape and size I desired. Not surprisingly, he was more than thrilled to assist in my research project.

"Yep, we need a bit more analysis. It's perfect! Just think, there'll be a bevy of knockers, right there in the flesh, for us to study. This way I can really get an idea what I want!"

"I guess, if you twist my arm," he grinned sheepishly.

"Shut up, you know you're dying to go. Let's go to the Skin Shop on Sunset."

"Are you sure you want to go to that one? There are way better places around town."

"How would you know?" I laughed.

"Duh, I know these things; alright, let's get this party started."

Dylan was fun, I really enjoyed hanging with him; it was easy, and we seemed to always be laughing. He was like hanging with a girl-friend…well, kinda, but you know what I meant.

Dylan was driving like a dork, because he was so buzzed. He was going about five miles-per-hour.

"Where am I going? I can't remember exactly where it is on Sunset."

"It's across from the old Carlos 'n Charlie's; I can't remember what it's called now."

"Where the hell is that? Carlos and who's? I haven't a clue what you're talking about."

"I mean Dublin's; it's called Dublin's now, or, wait, is it House of Blues? Now I'm confused. Keep going, we're almost there."

Dylan was cracking me up, he kept repeating over and over, "I can't believe we're doing this, you're wacked. Every time we get togeth-er it's out-of-control, the places we end up, the things we do!"

"There…THERE…THAT'S IT!

"WHAT? WHOA!!! AHHHHH, SHIT!"

We just about slammed into a car.

"What the hell are you doing, telling me at the last minute? I'm buzzed, for god's sake! You can't just yell *"THAT'S IT!"* and expect me to maneuver that fast. You could give someone a heart attack, for heaven's sake; you're one dangerous chick to hang out with."

Dylan was a little shaken, for good reason I suppose; this drinking and driving thing had to stop. Next time we needed to Uber it, no more wasted driving.

"Whoops, sorry…I was spacing out, and now we just passed it… there it goes. It's not the Skin Shop; it's called the Body Shop. I'm such an idiot. We can turn around and park behind it, the sign says there's parking in back."

"The Skin Shop, unbelievable, you're such a dork. I didn't know you meant this place, I was thinking of a different one."

Dylan was having a very hard time turning the car around, but a great time making fun of me.

"Dylan, I just remembered, isn't there some sort of rule about certain strip clubs serving alcohol and some not having any? We have to go to one that has alcohol, because if I'm going to be staring at titties all night, I want something to drink. Plus, I don't want to come down from this lovely tequila high."

Dylan seemed to know the difference.

"The all-naked places don't sell alcohol, but the topless bars do."

"Well is this all-naked or just topless?"

"I don't know, I've never been here before."

"Okay, then can you run in and see if they serve alcohol? I'll wait here."

"Why don't you jump out and check, I'm driving."

"Come on, please, will you just go in and ask? I'll watch the car; I don't feel like getting out…please…"

"Oh I get it, Sylvie, this makes tons of sense. I'm driving, but because YOU don't want to get out and ask, I'm going to illegally park so I can find out for you, while you sit and wait in the car."

"Right, exactly," I was cracking up.

"You're such a pain in the ass," he muttered, laughing as he was getting out of the car.

He returned, huffing and puffing, "They sell alcohol, happy now?"

"Yep, let's park."

"I suppose you want me to hop back in and do that too, right?

"That would be fantastic, thanks; I see a spot right over there."

"Pain in the a…"

All of a sudden, I felt a gas pain coming on. Not good timing. I needed him out of the car, fast! Why did this always seem to happen when I was confined in a car, in a restaurant booth, or worse yet, in bed with someone?!

"Okay, I'll finish parking, why don't you go ahead and get us a spot in line?"

"What? I *am* parking. What am I supposed to do, jump out mid-park and get in line? You're nuts. The line isn't going to grow in two minutes."

"No, I mean, yes! Now! You must get out and get in line NOW! Seriously, I hear it gets packed in there." That was a lie, I'd never heard anything of the sort. "I'll meet you in line."

"What's wrong with you? You're acting even more bizarre than usual. Are you really drunk? Are you okay?"

"Go, please!"

I couldn't hold it any longer.

"Out, come on, see you in a second."

He got out, mumbling something under his breath, and then I heard him giggling to himself.

I couldn't hold it anymore…OMG, it was a bad one. What the hell caused that? Of course, I had eaten a bean and cheese quesadilla— note to self: minimize bean intake when in mixed company. I hoped to god this wasn't going to happen all night. I joined him in line, and he looked at me with a strange expression on his face.

"See, I told you the line isn't that bad."

"Thanks, Dylan, for holding our spot."

Oh no, I felt it building again.

"Um, I think I left something in the car."

"I'll get it for you."

"No, no, that's okay; you don't know what it is."

"Well, you could tell me."

I couldn't stand it any longer; my stomach was in pain and starting to cramp. I must have made an odd face, because Dylan looked at me funny and asked, "Seriously, are you okay? You look like you've lost pigment."

I responded immediately, probably too quickly, "No, I'm fine. May I have the keys?"

"Sure," he handed me the keys, "just curious, what's so important?"

"Um…lip balm…yea…lip balm and Excedrin, I have a headache. I'll be right back."

I couldn't get away fast enough. I must have looked like a speed-walking crazy woman with clenched butt cheeks.

As I rushed away, I heard him laughing and saying to lord knows who, "She's wacky, that's why I like her so much."

I wanted to make sure I was a safe distance away before I let loose. Oh no, NOTHING, zero, zilch, damn-it! I waited too long. I could see it now, as soon as I got back the urge was going to return with a vengeance. What was I supposed to do? Maybe if the music was super-loud I could squeak one out without anyone noticing, although I'd hate to take that chance and get caught. How embarrassing!

When I returned, Dylan was in front, waiting for me again. No line, just Dylan loitering by himself in front of The Body Shop; what an amusing sight.

"So, Excedrin Queen, can we go in now?"

"Yep."

We got a table right up front. It was incredible, watching the women up so close. What I found kind of shocking and creepy was how some of the men sat completely transfixed, staring at the women totally expressionless. You'd think they'd be whooping and hollering, showing some type of excitement.

Dylan was watching me.

"You seem to be enjoying this more than most of the men in here."

"I find it fascinating. Okay, let's get some beers. How about you get the first round, and I'll get the next one."

"Sounds good."

The girls were dancing and Dylan and I were talking and laughing, trying to figure out which breasts would be best for me.

"Unbelievable! Look at the size of those wall-oo-kas! How does she walk around with those things?"

We were giggling, amazed at how badly most of these women danced—but I doubted anyone else was analyzing their dancing skills. As long as they kept moving and shaking all the proper bits, all was good in stripper world.

Some of the girls were on stage way too long, and after about five minutes I was ready for someone new and naked.

"Next, next!" I was shouting at the stage.

"SHHHHH, you're going to get us kicked out of here!"

"Dylan, I'm just messing around. They can't hear anything, the music is way too loud."

When it was my round, I realized I was a little short—damn place charged an arm and a leg for drinks! I had fifteen dollars, and the beers were ten each, so clearly I didn't have enough for two. I had to make some kind of deal with our cocktail waitress. A negotiation was in order.

When she came over, I started in, "Okay, I only have fifteen dollars and we'd like two more beers. How about if I give you a fifteen dollar tip, and you talk the bartender into two beers on the house because your good friends are visiting?"

"He's my bud, let me see what I can do."

As she walked away, Dylan burst out laughing.

"I can't believe you just did that. Just when I think you've totally lost the plot, you've got something else up your sleeve…incredible."

"Hey it's worth a try, what do we have to lose?"

She came back with two beers—BINGO!

"Thank you so much; I really, really appreciate this."

I handed her my last fifteen dollars.

"No problem, I might even be able to get you guys a couple more if you need 'em later," she called over her shoulder as she walked away.

"No way, no fucking way! I can't believe this! I go to a strip bar with a chick and SHE talks the waitress into giving us free drinks. This is like the Twilight Zone. Isn't it me who's supposed to be flirting with her, trying to get us free drinks? Something wacky is going on here."

"Dylan, it's just me working my magic…"

"That's it! I figured it out! She digs you! She thinks you're hot. She's a lesbian, that's the only possible answer! I love hanging out with you, I gotta say—you're a hell of a lot more fun than most girls."

"That's because I'm not most girls," I giggled.

After a couple more hours and another free beer, the show was getting a little stale—time to move on. I managed to trip over a chair on our way out, and let out an extremely loud yelp right as Ginger was dry-humping the stripper pole. Dylan and I broke into hysterics, and the whole place turned around to give us the stink eye. Ginger didn't miss a beat.

We were busting up all the way down the street, and I realized my gas was nowhere to be found—thank god. As we got to the car, Dylan came up behind me and wrapped his arms around me, asking softly, "May I kiss you?"

"NO!" I blurted out, before I could even comprehend what I was saying and what was going on.

Oh my god, what? That had come out of left field and totally threw me for a loop. We'd been hanging as friends, and I wasn't thinking of him in that way; at least, if I was, I wasn't conscious of it. I saw him as my best friend.

He froze, with a look of pure horror on his face. I wanted to take it back, I felt awful.

"No...um...I mean, I thought we were just friends." That, I must admit, had come out pretty lame.

"No, sorry, what I meant was...where did that come from? You totally caught me off-guard." Not a heck of a lot better than my first attempt.

He wasn't moving, I thought he might have been in shock.

"I can't believe you said that with such passion, 'NO!' Geez, I'm not *that* bad am I? If I remember correctly, you seemed to enjoy our make-out session on New Year's Eve? Am I missing something?"

I was having a hard enough time trying to understand my own feelings, so how the heck could I explain them to him?

"No, no, come on, it's not like that. I was just taken aback, totally surprised. I mean, we're best buddies now, hanging out all the time, and then out of nowhere you want to kiss me. It just threw me; I didn't mean to be rude and hurt your feelings."

"It's okay; I figured there was a fifty-fifty chance anyway. It seems like you aren't into me like you used to be, but I wasn't quite prepared for *that* answer," he paused, and tried to put on a happy face. "Should we go to your house now?"

"Sure."

The ride home was unusually awkward, which was sad. The incident was a total buzz-kill, and our conversation was stiff and weird—discussing traffic and the weather, yawn, yawn. We didn't even discuss breasts like we were supposed to, and my great high disappeared completely.

CHAPTER 28

Ten minutes into our uneasy car ride, he started sharing what was going on in his head. He told me he'd never stopped liking me, and was hoping that we could be more than friends. When we first started hanging out he knew I was going through a lot of old crap and didn't want to scare me off, so he had played it cool. The more he was around me, and the closer we became, the harder and harder it was just being friends; he wanted more.

I apologized over and over for being so rude, explaining that I was in shock and needed time to think about things. I also explained that for the first time I was really happy being alone, and was a little gun shy about getting into another relationship. He totally understood, and was cool with going slow and letting things play out as they should. That was about it for our drama, and then we were back on track, our usual joking selves.

"Geez, I know I'm short, but I felt about three feet tall when you turned your head and yelled 'NO' as loud as you could. I mean, c'mon, a simple, *I don't think so,* would have sufficed. Nooo, instead you shout it loud enough for the whole bloody neighborhood to hear. NO!!"

So true, we were laughing so hard that I couldn't breathe. "Well, you could've warned me, you dove right in."

"Warn you? How the hell am I supposed to do that? *'Um…excuse me…but I am forewarning you that I would like to kiss your lips. What I* mean is I would like my lips to touch your lips and then maybe I'd like to explore a bit with my tongue. How do you feel about that? Is that something you might want to do? Why don't you think about it and get back to me, thanks.' Yeah, right, that would work."

I was laughing so hard I was snorting. What was it about him that made me giggle so much?

"I know, it just freaked me out. We're getting along so great, and I don't want to ruin it. It's something we really have to think about, because if it didn't work out it could ruin our friendship. Seriously though, I'm really sorry."

"*You* have to think about it. I don't. I *know* what I want; I would like to be more than friends, I always have. I do understand that I've been thinking about this for a long time and you just got wind of it."

"Yeah, it's not like I haven't thought about it…it's just…"

"Wait a second, you know what? I've got to say, you've been giving me signals lately, little ones, and don't even try to deny it. You've been flirting with me."

"What? No, I haven't!"

"Yes, you have! I can't believe you're even denying it."

"I really don't think I have."

"Okay, whatever you say. I'm not going to argue about it. I feel moronic enough as it is. Let's just let it go and forget I even said anything."

Now I felt like a twat all over again. I didn't *think* I'd been flirting with him…had I?

"I don't know what to say, this feels so weird. I love hanging out with you, but now I feel totally confused. I don't want to ruin what we have. My track record with relationships hasn't been that great, so I'm a bit apprehensive. Let's think about this to make sure we're doing the right thing."

"Yeah…okay…sure…but like I said, I don't have anything to think about. You're the one who's confused. *You* take some time and think about it. I know what I want; it's you. I want you to be my girlfriend."

Now I felt like I was in the Twilight Zone—how could everything change so radically in one night? Things were so simple until a few hours ago. We were doing boob research, giggling, and having fun—now a drastic change had taken place, and we were at a crossroad.

When we got to my house, Dylan asked if he could sleep on the couch, as he'd done many times before. I gave him a comforter and a pillow and went to bed. Trouble slept next to him on the floor; she absolutely adored him.

Lying in bed, my mind was racing a mile a minute. Whether I liked it or not, things between Dylan and I had changed; we couldn't go back to where we were before. It was out there, he couldn't take it back. He wanted me to be his girlfriend.

Of course I had thought about Dylan and me together; he was male, hot, *and* my best friend. We'd become so close that I couldn't imagine him not being in my life, so the fear of things not working out overshadowed the relationship option.

I wanted a nice guy, so what was wrong with me? Dylan absolutely fit the bill, but then again, Josh-Simon-Jake…they all seemed great in the beginning too, and look what had happened there. Maybe Dylan would turn into a mess too—or did I just not feel worthy of a good guy? I needed to figure this out sooner than later; if I didn't give it a go, I could be missing out on an incredible relationship with my best friend.

I was in bed, buried in mental turmoil, and Dylan was asleep on the couch with a shattered ego, when out of nowhere, I started feeling a bit horny. How odd, where did that come from? Was it watching naked women all evening, or Dylan trying to kiss me?

Ooooooo, it felt naughty with Dylan in the next room, and I liked it. What if he walked in on me and caught me playing with myself? Ummmm, what a turn on…he would be shocked and so excited, with no option but to pleasure himself, watching me intensely…Omg…if he only knew…

Vvvvvvvvvvvvvvvvvvvvvvvvvrrrrrrrrroooooooooooommmmm…

CHAPTER 29

Dylan was gone by the time I woke up, but he had taken care of feeding and walking Trouble for me; what a sweetheart. I was sure he left early because he was feeling a tad awkward, which I was as well.

I decided I needed total relaxation to clear my mind. I had quite a decision to ponder; a massage was in order. I stopped into my usual spot; they had an availability, but not with Juan, my usual masseur. No complaints here, I was lucky to get in at all. I was booked with Lillie. She must have been new, because I'd pretty much tried everyone here until I settled with Juan. He was an accident, just like today; I walked in without an appointment, and he was the only one available. I was a little nervous about a guy massaging me, but I was so desperate I went for it.

It was the best massage I'd ever had. He had this tickle thing going that felt fantastic; most massages felt like I was getting beat up when they were working out the kinks. I told all my girlfriends about him, which was a huge mistake; now he was always booked and I couldn't get in!

An hour later, I was back in my car, laughing and shaking my head. I HAD to tell Dylan about what had just happened. I started dialing three times before I had the nerve to connect; yeah, things were awkward between us right now, but who else could I share this story with?

Dylan picked up on the first ring, and I launched right in. He laughed when I told him my beloved Juan was unavailable, but gave me his full attention when I started the strange tale of Lillie.

"So, at first, Lillie was giving Juan a run for his money; he could have been facing some serious competition! After she turned me over onto my back, she put cool moist lavender pads over my eyes…heavenly. She continued the massage and I melted into the table." I stopped for a big, dramatic pause, "And then things got WEIRD."

"As she was massaging upward on the front of my right thigh, she moseyed a little higher than I remembered anyone going before…her fingers fluttered lightly over my private bits!"

Dylan gasped theatrically.

"What the heck was that? It was so wispy that I figured it must have just been an accident. I had just dismissed it when she switched over to my left leg, and did the exact same thing! This was obviously no mistake! She wanted to finger me!"

Dylan was cracking up. "Damn, if anyone was going pull a maneuver like this I would have figured it would be Juan, not sweet Lillie! What the hell was going on?"

"Right? I could feel a sweat breaking out and my face turning bright red, but what I found extremely disturbing was that I was tingling from head to toe and wanted her to do it again! Well, sorta, but not really, mixed emotions—but I found myself kinda turned on, damn it! She continued the massage and stayed away from my hoochie, so I chilled out and figured she probably just had sloppy fingers and hadn't realized what she had done."

Dylan snickered, "Yeah, sure, happens to the best of us."

"I returned back to my Zen state as she massaged my arms, head, and chest, but just as I was slipping into a doze, she started massaging the front of my right leg, working her way up…and up…and up…all the way up—and this was no flutter! She aimed for the sweet spot, found it, and started massaging that as well! I mean, she was stroking that baby. I bolted up so fast that the lovely smelling lavender eye pads flew off my face and across the room at about ninety miles-per-hour, just as the blanket fell, exposing my bodacious bod."

"Wait a second, what the…?"

"Precisely, my dear Dylan. So she looked at me innocently, and whispered, 'Happy ending, don't you want a happy ending?'"

"What? A happy who?" Dylan was laughing and playing dumb.

"I was totally blown away. A happy fucking ending? Okay, I know all about happy endings, guys get them all the time, but me, a woman? Why would she assume I wanted one? I mean, I thought I was pretty tuned in, but I guess I'm quite naïve on this front. Apparently, women are getting "rubbed out" as well! The relaxation I *had* been feeling went straight out the window, and I was a nervous wreck—could I have been more of a nerd?"

Dylan was snorting, he was laughing so hard. "So, my favorite nerd, how did it all play out? What did you say?"

"I told her, 'No thanks. I've already got someone to take care of that…Are we finished then?'" Chuckling, he asked, "Big tip?"

"I gave her 15% instead of my usual 20%; she lost 5% for freaking me the hell out."

After Dylan finally stopped laughing, he said, "Thanks! I needed that."

"Yeah, me too…okay, thanks for tuning in, join us next time for brand new adventures!" After an awkward pause, we said our goodbyes. I needed more time to process, before I could even think of having the real conversation we needed to have.

I took Trouble for a walk and went to bed around 8:30; I was slightly depressed, not knowing what to do. My day had not worked out like I'd anticipated, so much for expectations…

CHAPTER 30

The next day, I stumbled innocently into my newest obsession. I was in the hair salon, pampering myself once again; it seemed to be a habit lately. When I got stressed and/or bummed I wanted to change my hair, bathe a lot, and get massages.

Just as Allison's assistant was ready to wash my hair, I came upon this unbelievable photograph. It figured, now that she was ready for me, I was not. I clutched the magazine as if my life depended on it, certain that if I put this baby down, someone was going to snag it. I was hoping for lag time after the wash, but no such luck; I went straight into the chair and Allison wanted to catch up. It was like when you're driving and hoping for a red light because you're trying to do something, but no, now all the lights turned green!

Now I had to do the customary small talk; don't get me wrong, I liked Allison, but every now and then I didn't feel like chatting. I just wanted to look at magazines and chill out. The salon was the one place I allowed myself to read crap magazines and not feel guilty about it. I wondered if Allison ever got bothered by the chitchat; I mean, she had to do it with everyone, all day every day!

When all was said and done, I rushed back to the sitting area. I settled into the comfy chair and found the photograph that had sooooo moved me. The caption read "Key West."

My infatuation with Key West got slightly out of control over the next week. Any spare moment I could grab, I was on the internet or calling realtors, getting information on rentals and jobs. I had the urge to escape—time for a change! I was obviously trying to distract myself from the real issue at hand…Mr. Dylan. I finally realized I couldn't run, I had to deal with it. Bugger Key West for now, I was going to stay in LA.

We continued on with our *friend thing*, but it was weird, not like it was before that fateful night. The ball was in my court, and until I decided what to do, the elephant in our world wasn't going anywhere; personally, I was getting pretty sick of avoiding it.

Dylan worked at CAA. Unlike me, he knew exactly what he wanted to do with his life. He got started in the mailroom and quickly fell into an assistant position, working for a high profile music agent. He was on his way to becoming an agent himself, and he loved it.

I snuck into the conference room at work to give him a call. "UH… yu…dooo…how…a…yu? I have demo fo you to leess-en."

"Excuse me?"

"I have demo tape. You listen fo me? *I give good music.*"

"I'm very sorry but I can't do…"

"WHY you can't? I good, you missing out boy…beeg time…" I couldn't help it, I started laughing.

"You twit, you had me going. I give good music, that actually wasn't so bad. I do think you've totally lost it, but I dig you anyway. So what's up?"

"I just wanted to call to say hi, and see what you're doing later."

"I'm here until at least 7:00."

"Let's get something to eat after…if you want to."

"El Coyote!" We said at the same time.

"Perfect, I'll see you at 7:30. Whoever gets there first, grab a booth."

He sounded very excited, which was reassuring because I was feeling a bit nervous.

"Excellent, see you then."

"Ta-ta." At last, I was ready to talk about us; 7:30 couldn't come soon enough.

I opened my front door and it slammed straight back at me, clobbering me in the head and almost sending me backwards down the steps. That would not have been good; what the heck was going on here? As I walked in, I realized Trouble must have jumped on the door just as I was opening it; she was so big now. Crazy girl—she was jumping up, down, spinning sideways and hopping backwards, about as whacked as her mom. I threw my stuff down and got on the ground to wrestle with her. She loved it, and licked my face clean. I got up, coated in dog hair and saliva—totally worth it.

"Want a biscuit?"

The mere mention of the word "biscuit" or "walk" sent her into oblivion. She practically bit my hand off, and ran straight into the bedroom to enjoy it on the carpet next to the bed, her special spot to enjoy her tasty treats.

When the leash came out, the antics started up again; she was moving so frantically that I couldn't get it on her. So bizarre—if only she realized this only postponed the walks. I was sure that wasn't her intent.

Once I wrestled her out the door, Trouble was even more bouncy than usual; I wondered what was going on in her little head. When I had found her, I actually named her Red; not too original, but she was such a beautiful reddish color that it seemed to fit. Due to her frequent shenanigans, I changed her name to Trouble, which fit her perfectly; Red was just tooooo boring for a girl of her caliber.

Our walk took on a whole other drama. Usually she was jumping on people and knocking kids down, but today it was a flirty cat that caused the ruckus. The cat ran right up to Trouble, making sure to get her attention, and then darted off. Trouble went ape-shit, tearing after that damn cat and pulling me along as well. I was totally off-kilter, and I tripped over a sprinkler and fell right in the middle of someone's front lawn. That didn't stop her, she actually dragged me a couple feet before my adrenaline kicked in and I was able to yank her back. OMG, how embarrassing, a grown woman who can't control her dog—granted she weighed seventy pounds now, but still! Sprawled in someone's yard with a dog jumping all over me, licking my face, I couldn't help it; I burst out laughing. Just another day with Trouble. Damn cat!

The rest of our walk was incident-free; thank god, because I'm not sure I could handle much more. On our way home, I contemplated what I was going to say to Dylan. I had no clue but I was sure it would come to me—or at least, I hoped…

(HAPTER 31

Dylan beat me there, and he had my margarita ready and waiting for me. I was feeling a bit awkward about what to say, and where to even start; all I knew is that I wanted to clear the air, so we could go back to the way we were before.

He started first, thank goodness. "I'm sorry again about *that* night, I didn't want to make you feel uncomfortable. I thought you might be feeling the same way, so I went for it. Obviously, I was mistaken. I didn't want it to ruin our friendship, but it seems like things have been pretty off between us, and I don't like it."

"No…no…don't be sorry, you're probably right. I've been thinking about this a lot, and if I'm truly honest, perhaps I was flirting with you. I mean, I love hanging out with you and I totally adore you, but I wasn't sure if I wanted to go to the next level; now I understand that's not fair to you. I suppose I'm just scared of getting into another relationship right now. The last few didn't go so well, and you're my best friend, so it makes it even scarier if things don't work out."

Wow, I surprised myself—where had that come from? I knew if I just relaxed, everything would fall into place. Dylan started smiling.

"Does this mean you *were* feeling the same way? Or that you *are* feeling the same way?"

"Well, I was selfishly enjoying the flirtation and not wanting it to go any further, because that's when everything seems to get screwed up…"

He took a sip of his margarita and responded, "What a distorted view of things. Just because you've had one or two bad relationships, um…well, uh, maybe a few more for you…" I laughed and kicked him under that table, "Just because they haven't worked doesn't mean all relationships will go the same way. Yeah, sure, it's a gamble at the best of times, but we have such an awesome friendship, so that puts us ahead of the game. Once two people decide to take things to the next level, that's when things start getting interesting and exciting."

"That's definitely the healthy way to look at things, but right now I'm scared to death of getting hurt again. But I also don't want to run away and pass up a possibly amazing experience."

"Sylvie, I don't want to hurt you. I saw how much pain you were in with Simon. I've been thinking about this for months, and *I* know how I feel about you; I've seen you gorgeous, sick, bitchy, grubby, bossy, hungover, pissy, all of it—and I totally dig you. Most relationships start by dating, so the bullshit stays covered up for ages, and then when the crap comes out its tough because a lot of time has been invested and it's harder to get out. It can take a long time to know someone the way we know each other. I know all of you…and I adore every bit of it!"

"Dylan, I had no idea, I don't know what to say…you know…um… why don't we give it a try?" Wow, not very eloquent. Talk about a woman of few words.

He slid into the booth next to me, putting his arms around me and asked, "May I kiss you?"

"Ummm…yeah…sure, I mean yes, yes of course!"

"Good answer." He leaned over and kissed me tenderly; it felt like a first kiss. I didn't remember it feeling this amazing when we kissed before—it was great, but not like this. Something was different; it felt very deep and sincere. It touched my heart.

The rest of our dinner was pretty amazing; he came clean about how he'd been feeling since *that night*. He revealed that he wasn't able to sleep, so he'd get up in the middle of the night to go jogging at the high school or go to 7-Eleven, just to chat to the guy working there. Too funny. I had a lot of respect for him, sharing his feelings and not trying to play games with me. I wasn't so sure I could be that forthright about such things…but I decided to start working on it…

After dinner, we went back to my place and sat around chatting and drinking beers. Trouble had loved Dylan from the first minute they'd met, and watching him roughhouse on the floor with her now made my heart swell. *This guy could be really great for both of us.* We were back to our normal *hanging out* selves, and it felt fantastic. When it was time to go to bed, he asked if he could stay over and sleep on the couch; perfect, I didn't want to rush things.

So much for that; the bedside clock read 3:03 through very sleepy eyes when he walked into my room and asked if he could get into bed with me!

"Wait! I'm not ready, isn't this a bit soon?"

"No, no, I didn't mean *that*. I just want to cuddle, I promise, nothing else."

"Okay, that's works."

He slipped in between Trouble and I, wrapping his arms tightly around me as we spooned. He snuck in a little kiss and nuzzled my neck, and I smiled. *This is lovely, I could get used to this.*

CHAPTER 32

After that evening, things between us were fantastic. We had some pretty intense make-out sessions, but I wasn't ready for sex; in fact, I was scared to go there. What was my problem?

My therapist and I started working through my intimacy issues, and once we started unpacking them, I was amazed to look around and realize how much emotional anguish I had been carrying around. Between feeling abandoned by my mother, and hurt for myself, my father, and my sister, I had built an adult life on the feelings of a scared child. Everything that brought Dylan and me closer caused me anxiety and fear. It felt way more terrifying with him; going from friends to lovers was freaking me out. I thought I would get over it once we started kissing, but then I started to worry about sex.

After a month of agonizing about it, I decided it was time; it had to happen, we had to sleep together so I could mellow out and stop the madness. I felt like I was a constant stress case; all I thought about was this damn relationship, one worry after another. This sex thing started to seem like the last obstacle before true happiness could be achieved. Dylan, on the other hand, was so amazing and patient; he never pushed. He knew that when I was ready, it would happen.

The scene was set; I stocked up on goodies for us to munch on, opened champagne, and put on Mazzy Star. It was exciting; even though we were sitting on the couch, drinking and laughing, not much different from any other night, I had wild plans in store for us that Dylan knew nothing about. After we finished the bottle of champagne, I felt a little squiffy; perfect, I needed a buzz for my plan, so time was of the essence.

I leaned over, gazing deeply into his eyes, moving closer to kiss him and then...I busted up laughing. *Unbelievable, what an idiot.* Uncontrollable hysterics set it, the more I tried to stop it the worse it got; there seemed to be no end in sight. Then I graduated to laughing so hard I was crying. This was *not* a good thing. Obviously, I wasn't using this buzz wisely.

Dylan looked humiliated. "What? This is great, just great, you lean over to kiss me and you lose it. What's wrong with you?"

Poor Dylan. This sucked; good question, what the hell was wrong with me?

"I...I...I'm so sorry, I'm buzzed and nervous and I don't know. It's not you; it has nothing to do with you. It's me, I'm an emotional mess."

"Oh no, nothing to do with me, of course not, it's me you're looking at."

"I'm really nervous, and when I'm super-anxious l tend to start cracking up—please don't take it personally. I'm so used to laughing with you that being serious seems odd at times."

"Oh great, odd? This feels odd?"

"No, not odd, Come here."

I pulled him close and started kissing him, and gratefully the laughter was nowhere to be found. I laid him down on the couch and smothered him with kisses, so he had no room for upsetting thoughts. I had a plan, so I turned him over; oooops, not as gently as I would have liked. Great, now he probably had whiplash.

I pulled out the massage oil I had hid under the couch and started to knead his back and shoulders.

"OOOH...that feels great. Mmmmm...oooh...right there, up by

the shoulder…ahhhhhhh…yes."

At last, all was going well; we were back on track. After a fifteen-minute massage, I attempted to gracefully remove his jeans—not an easy task. Dylan was moaning with pleasure until I started finagling with his zipper, trying to slip his pants off. I thought he stopped breathing, so I leaned down to kiss him as I threw his pants across the room. I was pretty sure I heard him exhale a few seconds later.

I worked my hands down his body, pausing to pay special attention to how amazing his ass looked in his old school, geeky-sexy tighty-whiteys. Dylan started moaning again. Between the bubbly and his body, I was feeling dreamy and aroused. As I was caressing and massaging him, I unbuttoned and slipped off my sweater. Slight predicament—it was a twin-set, and the other sweater was buttonless. It had to go over my head, which was going to be tricky with one hand.

Dylan peered over his shoulder. "Look at you…you're so frickin' beautiful. Kiss me," he begged, gazing into my eyes adoringly.

I pulled off my sweater, and Dylan looked surprised and very pleased to see that I wasn't wearing a bra. He pulled me close, kissing me, moving his way slowly down my neck and to my harden nipples.

I was so turned on it was crazy, how could I have ever feared this? I moved my hands down his body; I was on a mission, and I found exactly what I was looking for. It was impossible to miss, his huge, throbbing cock—hey new best friend! Wow, he was very, very excited—time for a different type of massage. Dylan was moaning and panting, obviously extremely pleased.

I slithered down and started to lick and kiss it—and then all hell broke loose! He was off like the bloody Fourth of July, exploding straight into my eye and then AGAIN, bam, wow; this kid has impeccable aim. Perfect bull's-eye ejaculation directly into my eyeball, he had some power behind that shot.

Ohhhhhhhhh, my eye was burning hellaciously. Thankfully, we were in the dark—I didn't want him to know what happened! He would surely feel like a total twit, and even I was wondering, *can't anything go smoothly with us?* I was sure he was wondering why I ceased all activity; granted he was over and done with, but that didn't mean I had to freeze, speechless, lingering in his crotch.

"That was unbelievable. Um, sorry, I guess I was a little too excited, come and give me a cuddle."

He pulled me towards him and started kissing me. My right eye appeared to be glued shut, but he didn't seem to notice. He had other things on his mind, like making sure I was fulfilled.

He gently rolled me onto my stomach and starting rubbing my back, while slowly removing the rest of my clothes off my trembling body. The only glitch was my damn eye; it was burning like hell. I couldn't rub it, I had contacts in. It was a little distracting to envision them slowly disintegrating from that potent, hardy sperm.

His hands were easing lower…and lower…and low…er…oooh! Mmmmmm…oh yum, how did he know, I mean how did he know so well…just the right pressure and brilliant circular movements…ohhhh…ahhhhhh…to hell with my eye…uhhhhhh—ohhhhhh—goddddddddd…AHHHHhhhhhhh. I was squirming out of control and went ridged. I had the most marvelous orgasm I'd had in a long, long, long time…well, at least without a battery-powered aid!

"Oh my, where did you learn *that* one?"

"Come here, you sexy vixen, *you're* amazing."

We snuggled, and I wondered how I could have been so scared; this felt so incredible and unbelievably comfortable. No more anxiety, I knew then and there that things were going to be just fine between us. We were ahead of the game; we had an awesome friendship, and now my fears were put to rest about the sex issue. I didn't see any clouds on the horizon.

The stinging in my eye came back with a vengeance; I had to get out of there and wash it before Dylan noticed. I jumped up with such force that he thought I was upset.

"What's up, are you okay?"

He raced after me.

"Yes, yes, I'm fine; there's something in my eye…"

I kept trying to look away, but he stepped right in front of me, staring in total shock.

"What the hell is wrong with your eye? It's HUGE and purple. Are you okay?"

He kept gawking at me in disbelief, which was totally embarrassing. I dashed to the mirror and couldn't believe how horrendous I looked. My eye was enormous, and the surrounding area was a combination of red, purple, and blue—it looked like someone hauled off and sucker punched me. How mortifying that I looked so ugly after such an intimate experience. Could I please just disappear?

"Did I hit you when we were rolling around? I mean, how could *that* have happened?"

"Uh, I'm not sure you want to know."

My contact lens was toast, so I took both of them out, rendering me blind as a bat. This was going to be pretty interesting, because it was my last pair, and my glasses weren't going to be ready until next week. Murphy's Law at its best.

"Why? What do you mean? What happened?"

"Your projectile hit me right in the eye…twice."

"NO! Are you serious?"

He started cracking up.

"I did this? Wow, that stuff must be like acid…to do that kind of damage!"

"Worse than acid, trust me. Your marksmanship is pretty impeccable, do you practice?"

I couldn't help it; I started cracking up. This would only happen to us, our first time together. We were nervous as hell, and then he shot me right in my eye. The more I tried to flush it out, the gooier it got—this damn stuff was like glue, and it wasn't going anywhere. I had no choice but to wait it out; at least the stinging had subsided a bit, but I still looked like absolute hell!

I got back into bed and cuddled up with Dylan. We laughed, rolled around, talked, and then finally consummated our relationship. I definitely got lucky. He was a wonderful lover: totally affectionate, tender, caring, intense, funny, sensuous, and he adored me. I was no doubt falling in love; I'd never felt this way before, and it wasn't the least bit scary.

CHAPTER 33

My vision wasn't a high priority for the next couple of days, now that Dylan and I had discovered the carnal side of our relationship. We didn't leave the bedroom the entire weekend, except to take Trouble on her walks—which Dylan happily did for me.

Our sex life was just as fun and entertaining as the everyday stuff. Without fail, whenever we were together, there was always some sort of shenanigans going on. Fun seemed to be easy and natural for us; even the most benign activities we shared were enjoyable. More importantly, our relationship was totally exempt from any head games— which was so refreshing. Just to round out the perfection, Dylan adored Trouble, and she couldn't get enough of him; the three of us had a good groove going.

Simon got it through his head at last that it wasn't going to happen with us, and that I'd moved on. It took a while, but we became friends— nothing more. He got a new girlfriend, Ashley, who seemed like a total sweetheart; sadly, I heard through the grapevine that he treated her exactly the way he had treated me. On some level, it was a consolation, but I felt bad for her. I was sure she'd figure it out like I did, in her own time.

It was funny/depressing because now that Simon and I chatted occasionally, I got to hear his endless complaints about her. Amazing, I was sure that was exactly how he used to speak about me. He moaned a lot about how he felt trapped because she wanted more, and he didn't understand her frustrations with him. I laughed to myself, knowing full well there was a whole other side to that story! He was, without a doubt, never satisfied.

Dylan liked him and didn't have any issues with our past, so we double dated every now and then, and I got to see Simon in action with her. It was cathartic for me, watching someone else re-live this relationship, and quite disturbing. Ashley was super-sweet—a little quiet at times, but after she popped a few she livened up and *never* stopped talking. Simon still tried to flirt with me, confessing how much he missed me, and I would just tell him to calm down. Sad for Ashley, but I couldn't save her; she'd figure it out soon enough. Maybe if we ever become really good friends I could enlighten her, but right now it was not my place…this was her journey.

I got a postcard from him recently, filling me in on his new gig. At the end, he started on about how he realized he blew it with me, and he'd lost the best thing that ever happened to him. Yeah right! I started thinking that maybe I should tell her, I would hate for that to happen to me and not know…although I had a sneaking suspicion it did. One thing I *did* know was that Simon definitely needed therapy. I sent him a card in response with my therapist's name and number on it.

(HAPTER 34

I was absorbed in a job I truly hate—cleaning the house—when Dylan snuck up behind me and kissed my neck. This was awfully bizarre, since I hadn't even heard him come in *and* he wasn't supposed to come over. He spun me around to kiss him and he was already naked and full aroused. I was embarrassed; I was so scummy, dressed in sweats, hair thrown up, and no makeup. What a sight—how could he even have a boner, considering how gross I looked?

As soon as I got over myself, I got into it. With my hands over my head, he pressed me up against the wall, kissing me passionately. He tried pulling down my sweats over my hi-tops, but it just wasn't happening, so he kissed his way back up to my breasts, pushing my sweatshirt up around my neck.

Things were definitely getting hot and heavy, and I was ready to throw him down and have a bit of him right there in the hallway. I tried to maneuver onto the floor, but he spun me around—he wanted me doggie style, up against the wall. My feet got tangled in my sweats and I fell in slow motion, pulling him down with me. How he managed to keep an erection through all of this was beyond me. We resumed action on the floor, but he had his heart set on the wall position. Getting back up was quite the challenge, but I made it. In retrospect, I had no idea why didn't we stop to take my clothes off properly; who knows, sex stuff defies all logic. We were back in position with my hands on the wall, and Dylan was thrusting behind me.

All was progressing magnificently; our breathing and momentum were in good form, but just as we were closing in on the finish line, Dylan started yelling and pulled away.

"Ahhhhhh! Trouble licked me! I can't continue with a dog licking my ass! It's too weird."

"Why not?" I joked, "Most guys would love that; hell, I've read about guys training their dogs to lick their balls and other stuff, you know peanut butter on the…"

"Yuk! Stop! Please! It's just too strange, I can't! It doesn't feel right."

There he was, naked and semi-erect, with Trouble sitting next to him, completely oblivious to what she'd just done. She seemed to enjoy when we were fooling around—I wasn't sure why, but she definitely did. Probably because she knew if we were excited and giggling, we were happy.

"Look at us, we're not right," I giggled, looking at Dylan's half-mast and my pathetic outfit. I started laughing so hard I was snorting, and then Dylan lost it as well. Trouble took advantage of the confusion, lunging at Dylan's manhood—she'd been eyeing it, but I never thought she'd go for it!

"Trouble, NO!" Dylan jumped back, tripping and falling over his shoe—that was definitely the end of his erection. He grabbed his undies, pulling them on quickly for protection. Poor guy, he was lying on the floor next to his red Converse with a defeated look on his face; his seduction plan hadn't worked out as he'd hoped, but we had fun.

I joined him on the floor, snuggling up next to him and smooching on his neck, hoping to make him feel better—which developed into a beautiful lovemaking session. I knew at that moment I was absolutely in love with him. I couldn't imagine being with anyone else, he was it.

Someone once told me that if you drive a Pinto all your life, that's what you're familiar with, so it feels comfortable. If you have a chance to drive a Rolls Royce, then it becomes pretty obvious what you'd been missing, and you'd never want to go back to driving the Pinto. In the back of my mind, I had doubted I'd ever find a Rolls Royce, so I kept settling for Pintos. Dylan was my Rolls Royce, and I had no desire to ever step foot into a damn Pinto again. I was one fucking fortunate chick. He didn't play games and he never took me for granted. Being on real, stable, and solid footing in a relationship for the first time ever, made me examine my own crazy behaviors. When we had a disagreement, I didn't need to push him away so he could "prove" his love to me by coming back. I could tell how he felt by how he treated me. This was not a boy I was going to have to threaten to run over to get his head straight. This was a man who helped *me* get my head straight.

"I love you."

"You do?"

"Yep, I totally love you. You make me laugh, you're my best friend, you're a phenomenal lover, you're totally hot and a sweetheart to top it off. I think you're one special, awesome, rare hunk of a man, and I love you so much. I can honestly say I've never been so happy with anyone in my life."

"Wow! I've been dying to tell you, but I didn't want to freak you out. I've been in love with you for ages, way before we even got together. I love you, sweetheart! You're one extraordinary woman, and I'm so happy that you're finally mine!"

He looked at Trouble and blew her a kiss, whispering, "I love you too, Trouble."

We were so exhausted after that escapade that we fell asleep right there in the hallway, all three of us cuddled together, with my sweat pants still wrapped around my ankles. Needless to say, the house never got cleaned.

(HAPTER 35

Everyone arrived on time with the exception of Simon and Ashley; Simon was running late, as usual. I was pretty excited and a little nervous; I had never attempted to throw a dinner party.

The menu was a rich three-cheese lasagna, garlic bread, Caesar salad, and apple tart for dessert, which I had made from scratch. Sounds simple, but it was a far departure from my usual chips and dip. That damn lasagna took a day to prepare and was taking forever to cook, much longer than the recipe said it was supposed to. Cooking seemed so stressful, I honestly couldn't figure out how people did this all the time. The trick was trying to juggle cooking times, so that everything finished in tandem. It wasn't working as I'd planned, the garlic bread was ready and getting cold...uhhh.

Lou was hanging out on the couch with her fiancé, Matthew. Yes, fiancé—since moving in together had been such a great success, he wanted to make sure she was his for life. He proposed in front of Brady's apartment, in honor of the night they first got together, at that infamous New Year's Eve party.

I was really happy for them, especially Lou; she wasn't as manic and self-centered as she used to be; actually, she was very chill and super-happy. Amazing what true love can do for someone.

Emma was sitting with Lou and Matthew, talking with her new boyfriend, my ex-impromptu-roommate Tyler! We had all been hanging out one day, and I asked Simon what ever happened to Tyler. I had run into him a couple times after he moved out, but then he seemed to disappear. Simon told me he was living in Sherman Oaks, working as a set designer. I thought it would be a brilliant idea to invite him out with us and Emma…I had this weird vibe about them together. Well, my intuition proved to be correct. They had hit it off instantly and had been together ever since; six months, with no signs of spoilage. Tyler was perfect for Emma, a mellow, together guy and yet wild enough to keep her interested.

I invited Pops and Florence; I hadn't seen them in a while. Through all my self-absorbed Simon-obsessed days, I'd really neglected my family and friends. It felt great to see them now that I was in a much better headspace. I was excited to share my happiness with everyone. They'd just arrived, and were chatting with Dylan in the living room. It was wonderful seeing them; it'd been ages since we'd all been together. Pops was seeing someone, finally. She lived in Florida, so he'd bought a place in Palm Beach and was rarely at home in Balboa anymore. Hmmmm, close to Key West—maybe Dylan and I could go check it out one day. I was so thrilled for him; it took a long time for him to get over the crap Mom put him through, but he was back to his old self. Seeing Pops happy put a huge smile on my face.

Everybody seemed cheerful except for Florence, who wasn't so thrilled. She had brought her actor boyfriend, Jacob; they had met a few months ago, and she was already totally fed up. Supposedly he was way too self-centered and had a roving eye problem. He had beelined to the couch to chitchat with Emma and Lou as soon as they came in, ignoring Florence—which totally infuriated her. What nerve, to treat my sister like that in my home!

Florence was stomping around behind me, moaning about him, while I ran around the kitchen and stressed over my woefully undercooked lasagna. After fifteen minutes of her bitching, the sound of her voice was giving me a full-fledged headache…my advice to her was simple, dump him. Yeah, I was one to talk—look at my sordid past.

It was a lovely scene; everyone was in the living room, chatting, drinking, and munching on pâté and goat cheese. Dylan was catching up with Pops and trying to get Florence away from me, because he could tell that she was driving me crazy.

At last, Simon and Ashley arrived. Ashley looked a little out-of-it; they'd probably been fighting. Simon had that puppy dog look on his face I'd seen one too many times before. Lord knows what he had done this time.

Finally, the lasagna was finished cooking, so it was time to indulge. I put everything on the table, and, I must admit, it looked fantastic. The lasagna felt like it weighed about twenty pounds! Everything was all laid out and ready to roll. I was quite proud of myself for putting this whole thing together, this was rare indeed!

Since I didn't have enough chairs for a proper sit-down dinner, we ate in the living room—on the floor, the couch, and beach chairs—a very relaxed soirée. Everyone was having a great time. Even Florence was laughing wildly, waving her hands all over the place and telling a story that was making everybody crack up.

All was going splendidly—plates overloaded with food, wine flowing, fantastic conversation, and Dean Martin crooning in the background, when, all of a sudden, there was a huge CRASH!

"What was that?"

"OH MY GOD, THE TABLE!"

"What!"

"It collapsed!"

No way! Part of the table was on the ground; it looked like a leaf broke loose under the weight of all the food. This was awful, all that work and it was all over the floor.

"There goes seconds, I hope you got all the food you wanted the first time." I had to lighten the vibe, as we stared at the devastation scattered all over my floor.

"What the hell was that? How could a table just willy-nilly collapse like that?" Pops jumped into action, crawling underneath to figure what the devil happened.

"It looks like the wood that holds the leaf in place pulled away and broke. It was probably coming loose for quite some time. Hmm, have you guys been having rumpy-pumpy on this table?"

"Dad!"

"Come on, I'm just kidding…well sort of…but seriously, I see glue under there; did you pay a lot for this thing?"

"No, actually it was dirt cheap. I got it at a garage sale."

"That explains it, maybe it broke once already and they glued it, but obviously with the wrong glue and not very well, or it may have been the twenty-pound lasagna that sent it over the edge."

"Geez, Pops; you're a real card this evening."

Everyone was laughing, and I was just glad the wine wasn't on there. It would have been a real bummer to lose all of our alcohol, and a disaster to clean it off the floor. I was planning several surprise toasts.

I attempted to salvage the lasagna, which had toppled face down, and by a miracle of all miracles, it was still intact! My heavens, this was some industrial Italian dish. I was going to have to sacrifice the top layer, with all the delicious hard crunch stuff, because it was covered with Trouble hair. Oh well.

The garlic bread was touch and go; it was too difficult getting the dog hair off every piece, so I just threw it away. It was easy, I could make more. Forget the salad; it was a write-off because Trouble was already gobbling it up.

Everyone was scurrying around, cleaning things up, trying to fix the table; it was mass hysteria, but we were all giggling about how it would only happen to me. My first dinner party and the table bloody collapses—at least it wasn't boring!

Pops gave me a hug, and said, "So you mentioned a surprise? You said you wanted to have us all over to tell us all something important."

"Okay, hold on."

I ran to the fridge to get a few bottles of champagne and more glasses.

"Dylan and I were going to tell you after dessert, but I guess it really doesn't matter."

I filled everyone's glasses with champagne and gave Dylan a huge smile.

"Well, a lot of you may not remember, but I've been writing a script for the last few years, and I finally finished it a couple of months ago. My boss offered to read it, and long story short…she loved it!"

"Congratulations! That's fantastic; I can't believe you didn't tell us sooner!"

Lou had a weird look on her face, she wanted to be the first to know about everything; I guess she felt a little betrayed.

"I didn't tell anyone except Dylan, it was my little secret. I didn't want to jinx it, plus I was waiting for tonight to tell everyone."

"What's it about? Am I in it? What made you start writing a script?"

The questions were coming fast and furious from all sides of the room.

"I got the idea when I was temping and had to read scripts and critique them. I couldn't believe what crap was out there, and I thought I could do better. I've always loved writing."

"What's it about?"

"Brilliant question! It's about a girl's life, her woes with men, jobs, friends, family, and pretty much all the crazy antics she deals with on a regular basis. I wasn't sure if it would appeal to the masses, but I guess it's the right time for this type of story. Hey, I'm not going to question it; I know I'm lucky that they love it!"

"That's incredible, congratulations! A toast!"

"Wait, there's more…"

Dylan looked over at me, smiling; I went over and sat on his lap.

"Dylan and I are moving in together. Things have been amazing with us and we're really happy. He'll move in with me for now, but we're thinking about buying a house together. Hopefully I'll get a nice chunk of change for my script, and Dylan has money saved. Who knows, maybe we can pull it off this year. We've got a phenomenal feeling about us and our future…well actually, Dylan, can I tell them?"

"Of course, why not, you're on a roll!"

"Actually…Dylan asked me to marry him a week ago, at our new favorite place…but I said no."

There was a gasp from someone (I think my sister) and a "what?" came from Lou's direction.

Simon actually broke the silence. "Wait, NOT El Coyote!?"

I laughed, "No, can't stop loving El Coyote, but I'm branching out—he asked me at The Little Door. I love that place, so romantic. And I didn't say no *per se,* I just explained I was a little nervous about getting married so soon. I think moving in is the logical next step. I'm sure we'll spend the rest of our lives together, but I don't see any reason to rush; I don't want to freak out and do something rash."

Everyone laughed; they knew me way too well.

"Dylan is the most amazing man I've ever met…besides Pops, of course." I looked at Dylan, "I absolutely adore you with all my heart, so we're going to live together first."

I was babbling and hoping it was making sense. Just talking and thinking about getting married made me feel all clammy and anxious;

the whole marriage thing kinda freaked me out. It was just that *fear* thing again, but at least I was working through it, little by little…

Dylan leaned over and kissed me.

"I love this woman; she's the most incredible, wonderful person I've ever met, and she makes me happier than I ever thought I could be. I'm a better person because of Sylvie, and she always puts a smile on my face. She's truly a very special, rare woman."

We toasted everything we could think of: the finished script, Dylan and I moving in together, all of us being together, our friendship, Lou's pending nuptials, Emma and Tyler, Simon and Ashley… that was a joke…my busted table, lasagna all over the floor, the salad stuck on Trouble's ear—basically anything and everything we could think of, just so we could keep sipping that lovely champagne…not that we ever needed an excuse to keep drinking!

We played Cards Against Humanity until one in the morning, and in the end everyone was thoroughly toasted. Pops was even a little squiffy, and he doesn't usually drink that much. During the game, Emma and Tyler disappeared for a bit, most likely for a mini make-out session, because when they returned with ear-to-ear grins and their arms wrapped around each other. Even Florence was lovey-dovey with her asshole actor. Champagne was certainly our love drug of choice. Throughout the evening, everyone kept telling Dylan and me how happy and content we looked together. Speaking for myself, I was so damn happy it was almost unnerving, like I was going to burst I felt so good.

I now understood what people meant when they said, "You know when you're with the right person." I used to think they were delusional. I knew, without a doubt, that I was truly in love with Dylan and that he was the man for me.

THE END

ABOUT THE AUTHOR

Sonia was born and raised in Southern California, living most of her life in Hollywood. Her mother was French, so as a result, her summers were happily spent traveling between Paris and Cannes. She eventually developed a love for all things European and returned to live in London as a young adult. *Losing the Plot in LA* is Sonia's first novel. She currently lives by the sea in San Clemente, California with her dog, Holly, and is working on her second novel.